Halfway Across the Street

A WEST TINDALE ROMANCE

ELLE WHITTAKER

LEMONADE
HEART PRESS

ISBN (print): 979-8-9909996-2-6

ISBN (e-book): 979-8-9909996-3-3

First Published 2024, Second Edition Published 2025

Cover Design by Ink & Laurel

Content Guide

THIS BOOK CONTAINS:

Adult language/profanity

Adults confidently owning their desire, and consensual
open-door sex scenes

Discussions of physical abuse by a parent (past)

Emotional abuse by a parent/family dysfunction

Parent death (past)

Contents

West Tindale, Montana

HALFWAY ACROSS THE STREET

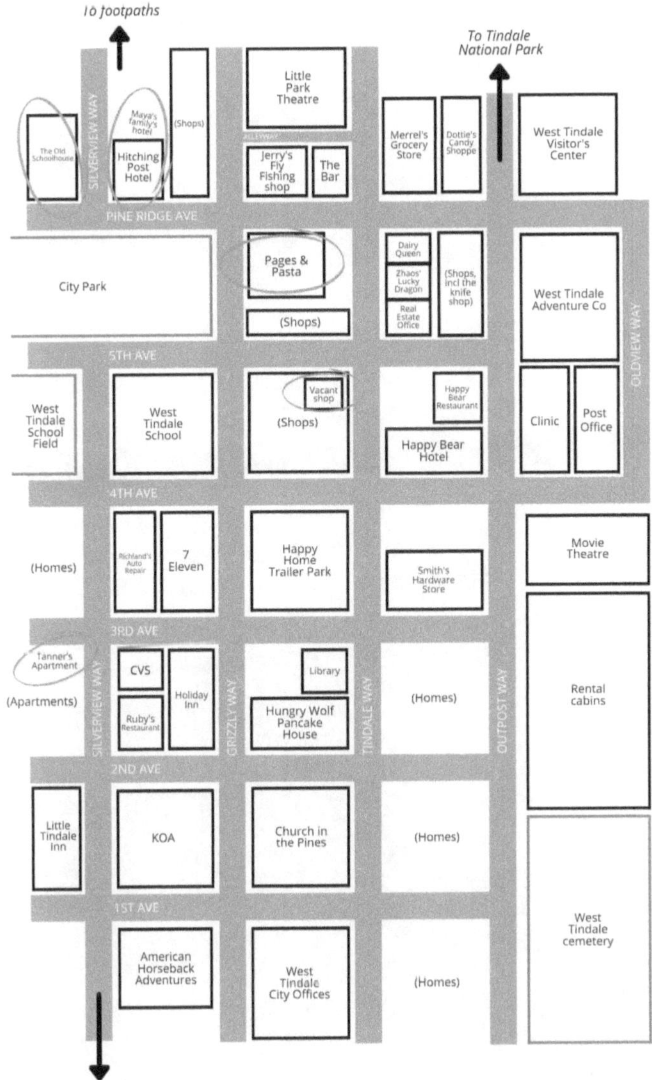

Tindale National Park

NOTE ABOUT INDIGENOUS HISTORY

Tindale National Park is a fictional place, based loosely on Yellowstone National Park in Wyoming and Montana. Indigenous peoples lived in that area for centuries before Europeans explored and named specific locations. Yellowstone was home to the Newe Sogobia (Eastern Shoshone), Cayuse, Umatilla, Walla Walla, Apsàalooke (Crow), and Tsètho'e (Cheyenne) peoples.

If Tindale National Park were a real place, it would likely share a similar history of colonization. The names of mountains, lakes, and other features would be the result of European occupation.

Out of respect for indigenous peoples, I did not wish to create an artificial Native American history for Tindale National Park to acknowledge. But I also did not want the history of colonization in this country to go unacknowledged.

I encourage readers to research the indigenous peoples who lived and continue to live in the places you call home.

For anyone who has ever had to re-learn what love is

CHAPTER 1

Drinks Are On Them

MAYA

Maya Clark wanted one thing only. She sat cross-legged on her bedroom floor and tried to clear her mind. After a few minutes, she lit the candle on her altar, took a deep breath, and closed her eyes. She spoke her next words in a reverent whisper.

"I call upon my ancestors, my higher self, and the universe in general. Tonight is my last night before shit gets real busy. So please, oh higher powers, please…let me get laid tonight." She took a few deep breaths, trying to envision the attractive stranger she'd meet, which was admittedly difficult, because they were a stranger. But whether from man or woman, Maya was determined to get some.

She had a roughly 70% success rate in manifesting a good hookup, and she hoped that tonight's spell would be enough to maintain that number.

Maya was a casual witch, since crystals and tarot and astrology brought her comfort, and none of it was actually harming anyone, contrary to what she had been taught in her small town elementary school classrooms. Maya was still meditating on getting laid when her mother's voice echoed down the hall.

"Maya?"

Maya sighed. "Just a minute!" she called back. She took another deep breath, then pocketed the carnelian and garnet stones from her altar and blew the candle out.

"Maya!"

Maya opened the door to her bedroom to find her mom standing in the hallway, about to knock. "Yeah?" she said.

"Are you good to go to the real estate office with us tomorrow morning?"

Maya frowned. "Am I supposed to go to the real estate office tomorrow morning?"

Maya's mom gave a half smile. She was wearing the long-sleeved button up shirt that everyone at the hotel wore, her collar perfectly crisp. "We want you and Devan to come, too. It's a big step for the hotel, and we think you two should be there."

Maya held back a frustrated groan. "But I already made plans with Anne for tomorrow morning. We're going to Silver Falls."

"I'm sure she won't mind."

"She might mind."

Her mother gave a sympathetic smile. "We're doing this as a family."

Maya sighed. "Okay. I'll let her know."

"Thanks, honey!" Maya's mom paused, then gave a quick up-and-down glance at Maya's outfit…jeans and a loose, flowing top, her tall strappy heels in her hand. "Are you going somewhere tonight?"

"I'm meeting Anne for drinks."

"Oh, how fun! Say hi for me. Don't stay out too late."

"Should I let you know when I come home? Like I'm sixteen?"

Her mom ignored her.

Maya grabbed her purse and closed her bedroom door behind her as she headed down the hall, fighting a wave of annoyance. First of all, she was twenty-eight years old, and while not paying rent was nice, it also kind of sucked to have your mom tell you "Don't stay out too late" on your way out the door. Second of all, it didn't make any sense to have both her and Devan at the real estate office tomorrow morning. Their parents were making an offer on the old schoolhouse, the building just north of the hotel, on the other side of Silverview Way. But neither Maya nor Devan needed to be there. The Clarks planned to turn the building into a restaurant connected to the hotel…another revenue stream, which would help in the off-season.

And they needed help in the off-season. Financially.

One of the challenges of living and working in West Tindale, Montana was that your entire yearly income needed to be made between May and September. Because the rest of the year, the town was practically snowed in. The Clarks, like every other local family, depended on the thousands of tourists that came through on their way to Tindale National Park. And when they didn't make enough during the on-season, they had to tighten their belts in the off-season.

Maya was no accountant, but she knew that even with a busy tourist season, the Hitchin' Post Hotel was barely staying afloat. Having a restaurant would double their income, and they'd been planning it for years.

Going to the real estate office didn't seem like that big of a deal to Maya, but when the Clarks "did things as a family," you didn't say no. It was *family*. And family came first.

Of course things weren't perfect at home, but Maya was raised to be loyal, and loyal she was. It meant living at home, even though she was twenty-eight years old. It meant getting a degree in Hotel Management so that she could come back to her small hometown and help her parents run The Hitchin' Post Hotel. It meant telling her best friend that she couldn't spend the morning going to Silver Falls with her because she had to go to the real estate office with her family.

Maya's annoyance faded as she opened the door to the bar and saw Anne sitting at their usual booth. Anne waved over the plate of fries already on the table. Maya slid into the booth and grabbed a few.

"Sorry I'm late," she said through a mouthful of food.

"You're good," Anne said. "I ordered you a red wine."

"I'm so glad we're friends," Maya said, grabbing another handful of fries.

"I'll drink to that!" Anne said, raising her Shirley Temple.

"I'd clink your glass except I don't have one yet." Maya raised an imaginary glass and mimed bumping it against Anne's. "The really dumb thing about this is that you're not even drinking."

"One of the downsides of breastfeeding," Anne replied.

"Speaking of, it turns out I can't come over tomorrow morning."

"Because of...breastfeeding?"

Maya laughed. "No, to help with baby Tommy. Apparently my mom and dad want the whole family to go to the real estate office tomorrow to make the offer on the old schoolhouse, which doesn't make sense to me but apparently it's a family thing. Are you gonna be okay in Silver Falls on your own?"

Anne sighed. "I might just save the Silver Falls trip for another day anyway. It's just so much easier with two adults, and Roberto can't always skip work. I never realized a baby would complicate everyday tasks so much."

"I'm sorry."

A waitress came by with Maya's wine. She was maybe in her early twenties, with short blue hair and a nose ring. Maya didn't recognize her, so she must be one of the seasonal workers who came to live and work in West Tindale during the busy tourist season. She smiled at Maya before leaving the table. She was cute.

Maya watched her walk away, then took a sip of her red wine. "I really don't want to go to the real estate office tomorrow," she said. She sat back in the booth. "It's really too bad that they don't give a fuck about what I want."

"What do you want?" Anne asked, grabbing another French fry.

"What I actually want is to get laid tonight," Maya said, sneaking another glance at the waitress behind the bar.

"Don't we all," Anne said. She paused, then added, "The waitress was cute. She gave you some lingering eye contact."

Maya grinned, then replied in a low voice. "I thought I caught a gay vibe!" She looked over at the bar, where the waitress was filling a beer glass.

Anne grinned back. "I'll be your wingman. Woman? Is it different if it's for something gay?"

"Definitely," Maya replied.

The two women had learned the waitress' name was Cora and were halfway through formulating a plan when a group of maybe a dozen men, all in various shades of camouflage, all wearing dirty baseball caps, had burst through the doors with enough volume to make Maya suspect that they were already a little drunk.

Maya hated these kinds of tourists. Obnoxious men who came up to the park to fish with their buddies, when what they actually did was just harass the wildlife and leave trash everywhere. West Tindale depended on tourism to survive, but Maya's teeth were grinding in irritation just being near these guys. Cora was quickly occupied with serving them.

After another twenty minutes, Maya glanced up at Anne. "I think tonight's a bust," she said.

"It doesn't have to be!"

Maya sighed. "I did a 'help me get laid' spell and everything."

"It might still work," Anne said. She glanced at the time. "Okay, how about I just get out of your way and you give it one last shot?"

"To be fair, I have given it no shots so far, but I like how you think."

Anne grabbed her purse and stood up, and after giving her friend a hug, Maya picked up her glass and made her way to the bar.

She was staring into her wine glass and wondering if she could get Cora's attention just long enough to get her number, when someone elbowed her arm.

"Hey, cutie," a voice slurred.

Maya looked to her left. One of the men had left the group and had come to sit next to her. He was maybe in his thirties, with dirty fingernails and sweat stains on his t-shirt collar.

"You from around here?" the man said. He was leaning on his elbows on the bar, his face far too close to Maya's. She could smell the alcohol on his breath and turned her face away. Maya was not about to tell this man that she was from West Tindale—the town was so small that he could easily find her. So she ignored him instead.

"I said do you live around here?" he asked again.

Maya thought about moving seats, but she was pinned between the man on one side of her and the wall on the other side, and the seats were taken all along the bar. Maya glanced up at Cora, who was down at the other end of the bar, trying to take and fill orders for the rowdy group of men. If Maya could just make eye contact, she could send an SOS.

"My name's Carl," the man said, his voice still sloppy. When Maya didn't answer, he added, "You're a very attractive woman." Maya cringed and tried to think of something to say that would get this man to leave her alone. She hated that her mind went blank in moments like this. In so many situations, Maya could come up with a witty retort or even an abrasive one-liner, but at times like this, her mind failed her. She felt like she was frozen.

"Is t'hard to hear in here? I said you're an attractive woman!"

"Hey," another voice said. Maya looked up to find another man standing behind Carl. This other man was… big. That was the only thing Maya could think for the first few moments she looked at him. Tall. Incredibly tall. What was this guy, six-foot-five? Six-foot-six? Barrel-chested. Thick thighs. Like a normal human had just been scaled up. He took up so much *space*.

"Yeah?" Maya finally said.

The tall man frowned at her. Maya noticed his eyes, piercing hazel above a…well, a frankly stunning beard, and even more impressive curly hair. "I was talking to this guy," he said, gesturing to Carl. He turned his attention to him. "I saw your gear out there. You guys catch any fish today?"

Carl turned in his seat. "Man, we didn't catch *shit!*"

"I was down near Roger's Pass this morning, but nothing was biting."

"We were up at North Lake all day, and our boy Bobby over there…"

Maya took a deep breath and tuned the conversation out as she took another sip of her wine. At least this Carl guy was leaving her alone now. She stole a glance at the tall stranger, who was leaning on the bar and listening to Carl ramble about fishing. Maya had never seen him before. She'd remember if she had. His eyes were truly striking. A mix of green and brown and gold that you could get lost in. Maya couldn't get over how big he was. Just a giant of a man. Like, a hairier version of the Brawny Paper Towel man. Or Hopper, from Stranger Things, but younger. Late twenties or early thirties, maybe.

Suddenly, he looked up and caught Maya's eye. He frowned at her, then his eyes flitted briefly to Carl and back to Maya again. When Maya didn't respond, his frown deepened. Almost into a glare. Like he was saying, *You won't give this nice guy a chance?!*

Well, fuck him. Fuck both of them. Maya downed the rest of her wine, then grabbed a napkin and scribbled something on it.

"Hey, Cora!" she yelled over the chaos of voices in the bar. The blue-haired waitress looked up, then walked over. Maya passed the napkin over to her. "I'm Maya. Text me." Cora's face broke into a grin, and Maya stood up.

"Oh, and these guys are paying for my drink," she added.

Maya turned to the two men, who were looking at her with something like shock on their faces.

"Thanks, boys," she said, and walked out the door.

CHAPTER 2

A Good Life

TANNER

Tanner watched as the brown-haired woman sauntered out of the bar. He was…impressed. That's the only thing he could think of to describe what he was feeling.

Well, that and turned on, but he decided to ignore that. Especially since she'd given the waitress her number and therefore probably wasn't into men. And also (he probably should have thought of this first), he had a girlfriend.

"Hell," the man next to him mumbled. Both he and Tanner were still staring at the door where the woman had just disappeared.

"Goddamn," the man said. Tanner thought he heard him say his name was Carl. "They don' make 'em like that no more."

Tanner cringed internally. He knew the guy was trying to pay the woman a compliment, but hearing him say it that way made it sound worse.

Based on what Tanner had just seen, this woman probably hadn't even needed him to come intervene with this Carl guy. (Carl, who was now talking incoherently about fishing lures.) Tanner just thought she had looked uncomfortable. He'd seen other guys step in by confronting whoever was being a problem, but at a young age, he'd learned that this didn't always work. It usually just escalated the situation. Things seemed to go more smoothly if you could just distract the guy until the woman could make her escape. Engage the aggressor, but in a casual way.

It was something he'd been doing for as long as he could remember.

Tanner nodded while Carl talked about how his buddy lost all their bait. He took a long sip of his Dr Pepper.

"Hey, what you drinkin'?!" Carl asked. "Let's get you another one!"

Tanner shook his head. "Nah, thanks, man. I'm heading out anyway."

He stood and got the waitress' attention, then paid for both his soda and the woman's wine.

Outside of the bar, Tanner pulled his jacket on and zipped it up. It was still cold in early May in West Tindale. He'd come here almost every year with his family when he was younger, but he had forgotten how cold the nights could get, even in summer. Those trips from his childhood weren't perfect—life in the Sullivan family never was—but most of his memories of *this* place were good ones. As he walked up Pine Ridge Avenue, he glanced up at the sky. He could never quite wrap his mind around how many stars you could see here.

Looking up now, he felt his lungs expand—it was so much easier to breathe when you weren't worried about keeping people safe. Having this much open space made it easier to just exist.

That was probably why those vacations with his family were so good when he was young. They weren't constantly pushed up against each other in a single wide trailer. West

Tindale Park was infinitely bigger than any house or car he and his family had spent time in. Even if you were sleeping in a tent in Tindale Park, you just had to unzip it and you had all this Montana sky.

Tanner glanced over his shoulder as he cut through the park and strolled towards his apartment on Silverview Way. There was the shop where he and his dad and his brother all got pocket knives one year. They had spent a whole afternoon sitting and throwing them into a stump, until it was too dark to see. Tanner must have been, what…thirteen? That would have made Billy eleven. Tanner wondered what had happened to those knives.

Over on his left was the bookstore where his mom always loved to go. Tanner studied the sign. It used to be called Winslow Books or something like that, but now the sign over it read "Pages and Pasta." And the Italian restaurant next door was gone.

If he really thought hard about it, it was a little insane that he was here…that he *lived* here. What he was doing with his life now had felt so far out of reach for so long. It was a pipe dream he couldn't even fathom saying out loud, let alone something he could actually make happen. But his father's life insurance policy had opened a door he didn't even know was there, and now he was walking through it.

He smiled at the buildings on his right, imagining his coffee shop among them. He wanted Sullivan's to be the kind of place that was a refuge. Someplace quiet and cozy, where people could feel safe. A little home away from home, a place to recharge. He pictured deep blue walls and bean bags and couches and a shelf full of books. Maybe they could even have open mic nights or something.

Tanner pulled out his phone and opened his notes app. He added "open mic nights???" to his list of ideas.

It was going to be a lot of work. Tanner knew that. And he knew it wouldn't be easy to do it all on his own. It was all of the work of both a major construction project and starting a new business. But Billy still had three more years of his sentence, and his parents were both gone, so it was all on him.

Tanner was almost at his apartment, still thinking about his plans for Sullivan's Coffee. He felt an unfamiliar sort of squeeze in his chest. He hadn't had a lot of experience with hope, but this must be what it felt like. Having something bigger than yourself to work towards. Not worrying about just surviving every day. If this was hope, it was a feeling Tanner liked, even if it made him a little nervous.

Tanner thought again about the woman from the bar. Was she a local? Was she single? But then he shook his head.

He pulled out his phone again and typed out a quick text message to Camille, still back home in Newcastle.

Just thinking of you, he wrote.

His thumb hovered over the keyboard. He wanted to say something more, but he couldn't think of what, so he just hit send. He smiled when his phone rang a few minutes later, but didn't recognize the number. He picked up anyway.

"Hello?"

"Hey, it's me."

"Billy?" Tanner frowned as he hung his keys on the hook by the door. "How are you calling me?"

"Cell phone," Billy replied, his voice low.

"How the hell did you get a cell phone inside a prison?" Tanner asked.

Billy was quiet for a moment before replying. "Dude, do you not understand how prison works?"

"Dude, do *you* not understand how prison works? You'll get in trouble if someone finds you with a cell phone." Tanner put his brother on speaker and pulled off his coat.

"Don't worry about it."

"How am I not supposed to worry about it?" When Billy didn't answer, Tanner sighed and asked, "Fine. How are you?"

"Good, man, thanks for asking. That's what I called for. You out in West Tindale?"

"Yep. Gonna buy the building tomorrow morning, and then start renovating."

"You gonna do it all yourself?" Billy asked.

Tanner walked into his kitchen and opened the refrigerator. "Who else is going to?" he said.

"You could hire someone."

"With what money?"

"Didn't you get a shit-ton of money from the insurance?"

"Yeah," Tanner said, grabbing a Dr Pepper from the fridge and walking into the living room. "But it all has to go towards supplies and the building itself."

"I'm just saying," Billy replied. "You don't have to do everything yourself all the time."

"I know," Tanner said, sitting against the wall and taking a sip from his drink. He still hadn't had time to get a couch yet.

Billy didn't answer, and Tanner could hear some sort of muffled movement on the other end of the line.

"Shit, I gotta go," Billy finally said. "Talk to you later."

"Bye. Get rid of the cell phone, shithead," Tanner said affectionately.

"Fuck off."

The line went dead. Tanner glanced at his phone, then sighed. Billy had been in California State Prison Solano for a year, but this was the first time he'd ever used a contraband cell phone. At least to call *him*. Billy was lucky. The judge had taken it easy on him since it was technically his first offense, although Billy had been getting into trouble since he was a kid. But this one was a felony. It was the first time he'd been caught fighting, and the fighting was bad enough to get the police involved. "Aggravated assault" was the official charge. He'd had a knife with him, and cocaine. He could have gotten *nine* years. Tanner squeezed his eyes shut and ran a hand over his face, thinking about what that would have meant. Four years was a little more doable, especially if Billy could get out early.

The last time Tanner had seen Billy in person was at their dad's funeral. Billy had been granted an escorted leave. It was awful…hardly any family, Billy there in a second-hand suit with some guy in a uniform standing behind him at all times. Tanner hated himself for thinking it, but after all that, getting to West Tindale had been…a relief. A new beginning.

God, that girl from the bar earlier was pretty. Tanner couldn't stop thinking about her. He glanced around his mostly empty living room. He'd have to get some furniture, and soon. Otherwise Camille would hate it here when she visited. A few boxes were stacked in the corner, and his mattress was on the floor in the other room. There was no table, no nightstand, no chairs. Just a set of weights on one side of the room, next to the boxes. It was fine for him— any extra money he had, he wanted to put into the coffee shop. But he'd definitely have to do a little decorating before she came out to visit. And if she decided to move here with him, then they'd definitely need to make some adjustments.

Tanner finished off his Dr Pepper and stood up. He stretched, his fingers brushing the ceiling above him. Even though it was a small, one-bedroom apartment, it felt huge to him. It was the first time in his entire life that he'd ever had his own place. He threw his soda can away and looked at the checkbook on the counter. "Sullivan's Coffee" was printed in the corner. He smiled to himself. Tomorrow he'd buy the building, and then he'd get to work. He'd finish renovations by the end of the summer, and then he had the winter to set up all of the food and drink details. This time next year, he'd be running a coffee shop in West Tindale, Montana.

He hadn't always been able to take care of the people in his life, but maybe this was what he could do now. Use some of his father's life insurance money to build a business, one that could support both himself and his brother. He could give Billy a job when he got out. He could build a life here. A good life.

It might not look like the life that everyone else pictured, but it would be a good life for him. It was already more than he had ever hoped for.

CHAPTER 3

The Real Estate Office

MAYA

Maya Clark was not a morning person. She thought of this every single morning that she had to get up before 10 am. So leaving the house at *7:50* am to go somewhere she didn't even want to go was a complete nightmare.

Maya, her brother Devan, and their parents Bruce and Harriet, all began the short walk a block south and crossed the street to be at the real estate office right when it opened at 8:00. Maya was clutching an enormous coffee and frowning at everyone and everything. Devan was also actively scowling. At twenty-three, he was only five years younger than Maya, but at this early in the morning, both of them turned into surly teenagers. Bruce and Harriet were unbothered by their children's lack of enthusiasm.

Halfway to the real estate office, Maya's mother stopped. "Wait! Let's go back and take a picture in front of the old schoolhouse!"

"Why?" Maya asked.

"So we can have before and after photos of the family in front of the building!"

Devan frowned. "If the before is before the renovation, can't we just do the before photo after we buy the place?"

"No," Harriet replied. "I meant before and after we buy it!"

"Mom, are you sure?" Maya asked. "It will look exactly the same."

"Don't talk back to your mother," Bruce said.

"I'm not talking back," Maya said. "I'm just pointing out that it makes more sense to take pictures before and after the renovation."

"We can do that, too!" Harriet said.

"Kids, come on," Bruce said. "Your mom wants a picture."

Maya resisted rolling her eyes as the entire family turned around and walked back up the block to the old schoolhouse.

Devan fell into step behind Maya and whispered under his breath. "Does mom also realize that this is going to make us late to the real estate office?"

"I didn't want to come in the first place," Maya whispered back.

At the old schoolhouse, Harriet adjusted her children's hair, and made Bruce take roughly 40 different selfies of the group.

"Smile, honey," Harriet said on their last picture, elbowing Maya.

"I am," Maya replied through her teeth.

Harriet squeezed Maya's hand. "I'm so excited we get to do this together."

"Take pictures?" Devan asked.

"No, buy the old schoolhouse," Harriet replied. "Your father and I spent so long building this business. And we did it for you. All of it was for you two kids. And now you get to know what it feels like to build on something, too. We get to do it as a family."

Maya felt her stomach give a subtle lurch. She thought of the years she spent at college, getting her degree in hotel management, sneaking in a figure drawing class when she could fit it into her schedule, just to keep herself sane. Working in art department's pottery shop part-time, even though she was taking 20 credits some semesters. But for the Clarks, family came first. And Bruce and Harriet really had built it all up from nothing…first the hotel, and now the restaurant. So a degree in hotel management was the least Maya could do. She squeezed her mother's hand back, then started walking with them back down the two blocks to the real estate office, throwing her empty coffee cup in a trash can on the sidewalk.

Maya reached the door of the real estate office first and started to pull it open.

"I told you pictures would make us late," Devan said from behind her. "It's already 8:10."

"Who else is going to come here this early?" Maya said over her shoulder.

And then she walked straight into what felt like a wall.

It took her a moment to get her bearings, but she slowly became aware of two hands on her upper arms, steadying her. She was face to face with a wall of plaid.

"Okay?" a low voice said.

Her gaze traveled upwards. Tall. Beard. Hazel eyes.

"You," she said. It was all she could think of to say. It was the man from the bar last night. His hands were still on her arms, and he was frowning at her. Maya felt frozen in place. And also kind of…warm? The feeling of his large hands on her arms wasn't totally…unpleasant. But then she remembered the disapproving frown he had given her when she rejected the creep at the bar the night before, and she immediately found the strength to pull her arms out of his grasp.

Neither she nor the man moved, but stood a few feet apart, looking at one another. Maya was suddenly very aware of her breathing.

Devan's voice finally broke the silence. "Is this… someone you know?" he asked.

"Nope," Maya replied, and she brushed past the stranger and walked into the real estate office, her family following behind her.

"Hi, Ruby!" Harriet said.

The woman behind the desk blinked in surprise. "Hi, Harriet! Bruce. Devan and Maya. Did we…have an appointment?"

"We didn't," Harriet said, sitting herself down in the seat across from Ruby. "We've wanted to keep it quiet until we were sure we could do it, but today's the big day." Maya stood off to the side, feeling a little disoriented from bumping into the man from last night. He was so…tall. And okay, fine, he was handsome. Like, really handsome. Even more handsome in the daylight than he was in the bar. Which was annoying. Maya shook her head and turned her attention back to the conversation.

Bruce stood behind his wife and rested his hand on her shoulder. "We even brought the whole family to be a part of this!" he added.

"What's the occasion?" Ruby said.

Harriet smiled. "Well, you know how stretched thin we all get in the off-season. We've been talking for years about starting a restaurant, and now we're finally ready." Harriet reached into her purse. She pulled out a check, then laid it on the desk in front of Ruby. "We'd like to buy the old schoolhouse, please."

Ruby looked at the check, then back at the Clark family

assembled before her. Then she looked back down at the check, staring at it for a long, long time. Finally, she looked up again, a stricken expression on her face.

"Harriet, I wish you'd told me," Ruby said.

"I know," Harriet replied, still grinning. "But like I said, we weren't sure if we could swing it, so we didn't want to make an offer until everything was certain. But the bank approved our loan, so here's the down payment!"

Ruby took a moment to reply. "I mean, I understand that. But I wish you'd told me you were interested. I could have…it's just…the old schoolhouse is no longer for sale. It's…it's already been sold."

No one said anything for a full ten seconds. Maya looked at her parents. Both Bruce and Harriet were staring at Ruby with confusion, smiles half-frozen on their faces. Devan was looking at the ground, his hands in his pockets.

Finally, Harriet spoke. "The old schoolhouse?"

Ruby nodded.

"Who bought it?" Bruce asked. "When?"

Ruby looked truly stricken. "A man named Tanner Sullivan," she said. "This morning. Right before you got here."

"Who the hell is Tanner Sullivan?" Bruce asked.

Ruby glanced over the Clark family's shoulders, her eyes resting on the tall figure still standing outside, his eyes on the phone in his hand. Maya's eyebrows flew up.

"*That* guy?" she said. The whole family turned to look at him. He didn't notice.

"He's new in town," Ruby replied. "Apparently he's going to turn the old schoolhouse into a coffee place."

Maya looked at her parents and saw the reality of their crushed dream slowly sinking in, disappointment making their shoulders sag. And she knew it was only a matter of time before that crease of worry appeared between her father's eyebrows. Maya didn't have to look at the hotel's books to know that they were barely staying afloat. And now to have their additional revenue cut off? She was suddenly filled with a fierce, bright hot anger. She glared at the man outside, who had just put his phone in his pocket and begun walking away. She wondered if the strength of her look could burn holes in the back of his coat.

"Are there…are there any other buildings zoned for food service available?" Bruce asked. Even if there was something, it would be harder to manage from the other side of town. Not impossible, but definitely not as convenient as a building right on the other side of the street.

Ruby shook her head. "I'm so sorry."

Finally, Harriet sighed, then spoke with exaggerated cheerfulness. "Well, I guess we'll have to change our plans! We'll come by again in a few days. Or we'll…call you." She stood up, grabbing the check from the desk and putting it back in her purse.

"Thanks, anyway, Ruby," Bruce said. Maya thought she saw her mother's eyes welling up as she turned away, but she was soon smiling with a manic kind of brightness, any trace of tears gone.

"Good to see you, Ruby!" Harriet said over her shoulder, as the whole family exited the building and stepped back out into the street. It was quiet as they all walked back towards the Hitchin' Post Hotel.

The man, Tanner Sullivan, was walking ahead of them, about a block away. Maya wanted desperately to catch up to him, punch him in the face, and then demand that he sell the old schoolhouse to the her family. And come to think of it, he probably deserved being punched in the face for defending that creep in the bar last night, too. Maybe she'd hit him twice. Then her brother spoke.

"I hate to say I told you so…" he began.

"Devan," Bruce warned.

"I'm just saying, if we hadn't turned around to take a bunch of worthless pictures, we would have gotten to the real estate office on time."

"The pictures aren't worthless," Harriet said.

"They kind of are. Now we just have a bunch of pictures of our family in front of a building that we *don't* own."

"Devan, don't be rude," Bruce said.

"I'm not being rude! I'm just saying we could have gotten to the real estate office on time!"

"Okay, well, I guess I'm just a horrible mother," Harriet replied. "Wanting to do something special as a family."

"Oh my god, Mom," Devan said. Maya could practically hear him roll his eyes.

"Why are you always trying to make me feel bad about things?" Harriet continued. "It feels like you're always guilt-tripping me about things I have no control over!"

Devan didn't look at Harriet as he replied. "You were the one who tried to get us all up to be the first ones at the real estate office, and then you were the one that made us late!"

Maya tuned her family's arguing out. As soon as Harriet played the "I'm a horrible mother" card, Maya never knew what to say. All she knew in this moment was that the jerk walking a block ahead of them had taken a dream of her parents' and crushed it. And not just a dream, a necessary thing for their family's financial survival. Her parents weren't perfect—far from it—but Maya was a Clark, and if you hurt one Clark, you hurt all of them.

When they got back to the hotel, Bruce and Harriet went into their office behind the front desk and shut the door. Devan slammed drawers as he set up for the day, taking over the desk clerk from the overnight shift. Maya wasn't scheduled to work the desk until later that night, so she took the stairs up to her room. Maya closed her door and collapsed onto her bed. She pulled out her phone and found a message from Anne.

> Congrats on the old schoolhouse! Tommy celebrated for you by having the biggest diaper blow out in the history of babies. Did you get laid last night?

Maya smiled in spite of herself.

> Atta boy, Tommy. I did not get laid last night, but boy have I got things to tell you. Can I come over later in like, an hour?

> Will you change diapers? I've met my quota of poop for today.

> What are godmothers for?

Maya put her phone away, and then laid in bed, thinking. After a few minutes, she reached over to her nightstand and grabbed her deck of tarot cards.

CHAPTER 4

Memories

TANNER

Tanner walked straight from the real estate office to the old schoolhouse. He was still thinking about the girl from the bar last night, the way she'd walked right into him this morning. He had been surprised to see her, her brown hair falling over her shoulders, her warm choco-latey eyes gazing up at him. He hadn't meant to hold onto her the way he had, but first he was making sure she didn't fall and then she was just…gorgeous, and he sort of froze.

She was even prettier in the daylight.

He had been about to ask her name, but then she'd brushed past him so quickly that he didn't have the chance. And she didn't seem particularly friendly, which was…fine. It's not like he even knew her. Or like he was looking to know her. *I have Camille*, he thought, a guilty twinge in his chest.

They'd been together for a year, and he had been reluctant to go long-distance. But Camille had given him that kind smile of hers and told him that he should take this opportunity and run with it. They made plans to visit each other at least once a month, and she was coming out to Montana for the first one in a few weeks.

When Tanner reached the old schoolhouse, he stopped for a moment and looked up at the building. He felt a smile slowly spread across his face. He couldn't quite believe it was his. He pulled the key out of his pocket and walked to the front door.

The door of the building was old, and it creaked when Tanner opened it. It felt like it hadn't been opened all winter, like the snow and cold of the past months had seeped into the wood. Everything was covered in a fine layer of dust.

The woman at the real estate office had said that the building had been a school from the early 1900s to the 1980s, when the new school had been built a block to the west. The city occasionally used this space for storage or community classes, but it hadn't been used very frequently. It had been empty during every year that Tanner and his family had come to West Tindale.

He'd always loved this building. His mom, too. The outside still retained its early 1900s facade, and his mom always went out of her way to visit it every time they came to West Tindale. She said there was something magical about it. When Tanner was little, he didn't know what he meant, but after enough time, it became magical just because she said it was.

There was one summer when Tanner was maybe fifteen…his dad had gotten a construction job in Nebraska, and for one glorious month, it was just Tanner and Billy and their mom. She'd thrown all of their camping gear into their station wagon and they'd road-tripped out to West Tindale, where they'd stayed for a week. It was late July, and there was a day when the three of them were walking down Pine Ridge Avenue, eating ice cream cones.

A freak thunderstorm had come up, a sudden torrent of warm rain sending everyone into shops and under awnings. Tanner and Billy and their mom had been right next to the old schoolhouse, so they'd run to stand in the shelter of its porch roof, the three of them huddled on the front steps.

~

JUNE SHOOK out her hair and laughed. She laughed so rarely that it sounded like music to Tanner. She held up her ice cream cone.

"I've never had an ice cream cone get rained on before," she said.

"I dropped mine when we started running," 13-year-old Billy said, pointing towards the sidewalk where his ice cream was now being washed away.

"You can have mine," Tanner said, handing his over. Billy took it and grinned. Tanner leaned against the front door of the building and was surprised to find it give way. He stood up straight and looked with surprise at the door behind him, now open a crack.

June looked at the door with wide eyes, then smiled at her sons.

"Come on," she whispered, and after Tanner and Billy grinned at each other, the three of them pushed the unlocked door open and slipped inside the building.

The room was dim, windows along two walls letting in a little of the gray light from outside. The rain pattered hard on the roof above them. The whole room smelled like sawdust and paint, and aside from a few empty cardboard boxes and the odd tool here and there, the room was empty.

June wandered towards the windows, eating her ice cream as she looked out on the storm. After a few moments, she turned and looked back at the room.

"This would make the perfect little cafe," she said. "Or a... coffee shop. Or something."

Tanner looked around, trying to see what his mother saw.

"You could have the counter over there," she said, pointing, "and little chairs and tables all throughout here. Maybe a big comfy couch by the window." June sighed with a sad little smile. "Imagine sitting next to these windows in the rain, reading a book and sipping something warm."

"You could have a shelf of board games over there," Billy added, pointing to another wall, the ice cream cone Tanner had just given him almost gone.

"And a big fireplace over here," Tanner said.

It was a game the three of them played now and then…quietly daydreaming, trying on a world that all of them knew they could never actually build. It was rare, these glimpses into some different reality, one where they had enough money all the time, and not just when their dad had gotten a good job. One where they could sit and watch the rain while reading a book, without worrying about what would come next.

None of them ever acknowledged what they were doing in those moments, the way they always chose dreams so impossibly big that they had to be pretend. But they did it anyway, just to prove that they could. Something quietly transgressive that they did just to see what it felt like.

Tanner, Billy, and June all stood in the echoing space, listening to the rain, taking in the rough wooden beams above their heads, the hard, dark flooring, the whitewashed walls. After a few minutes, sunshine broke through the windows and the rain stopped as suddenly as it had begun.

June smiled at her sons, then walked towards the door. "Come on," she said. "Let's get out of here before we get in trouble."

TANNER OPENED his eyes and looked around him. Were those the same cardboard boxes that had been here that day, more than a decade ago? Tanner wouldn't have been surprised.

He stood in the middle of the big empty room and looked around. It occurred to him that he probably should have come to look at the place before he bought it. He hadn't paid for an inspection or anything. He could be pouring a lot of time and money and energy into something that would never pay off. For all he knew, the foundation was rotting, or the windows would need to be replaced.

But the real estate office said the building was in "working condition," and Tanner trusted that the phrase meant "not condemned."

He made a mental note to have an inspector come out anyway, then began to gather the cardboard boxes and other small pieces of trash. He found a few cigarette butts in one corner and felt a surge of overpowering anger. He clenched his fists and closed his eyes until it passed.

Tanner hated those moments. Moments when white-hot rage flooded him and he felt like he had to stay perfectly still or else he'd break something. And most of the time, it was for the stupidest, smallest reasons. He couldn't explain why a few cigarette butts made him want to scream. Sometimes it was someone cutting him off in the road, or maybe he would drop a hammer, or the grocery store would be out of something. He'd be breathing normally and then all of a sudden, he'd feel like an enormous fist was reaching into his chest and squeezing his spine.

He had two scars on his right hand. One was from construction, a staple gun he wasn't paying close enough attention to while he was using it. That one was barely visible.

The other was from punching right through the cheap

wall of his family's trailer, scraping the side of his hand on the corrugated metal from the outside. It was the same year that he and his mom and Billy had explored the old schoolhouse. That fall, Len—he had stopped calling him "dad" years earlier—had grabbed Billy by the hair and smacked his head into the coffee table. Tanner had started yelling, and their mom had told him to be quiet and go to his room. Tanner had punched the wall until he could see the outside, until blood was running down his arm. His mom had come in and found him. They sat in the bathroom together while she bandaged him up, both of them crying, neither of them saying a word about any of it.

Thinking about those moments scared the shit out of him. Like there was some kind of monster inside of him that was one moment away from taking over him completely. He didn't hit people. But he knew the power to do it was there, coiled in his muscles. When he felt that rage come over him, he gritted his teeth and waited for the feeling to slowly fade away.

He knew he wasn't alone. Plenty of kids grew up in volatile homes. He knew so many people who had had it so much worse. The first time Camille had used the word "abusive" to describe his home life, he'd brushed her off, telling her that no one ever took a belt to him or put cigarettes out on his arms. Len was just a jerk, who had a temper. Everyone loses their temper sometimes. But Camille had traced the scar on his hand and whispered that a man grabbing his child by the hair and slamming them into a coffee table was abusive.

Tanner still didn't like the word. It didn't feel accurate. He hated Len for what he'd put their family through, but he couldn't bring himself to say that he'd been "abused." That he and his mom and brother were victims.

Although he supposed they weren't anymore, anyway.

When Tanner was told that Len had died suddenly of a heart attack on a job site, he hadn't felt…anything. And then he'd felt guilt about not feeling anything. And then he'd felt…relief.

Losing his mom had been so much harder, and it had been years before. Tanner hated seeing the way his mom seemed to get smaller and smaller in that bed, surrounded by tubes and monitors. He still hated hospitals.

In the dusty light of the old schoolhouse, Tanner shook these thoughts out of his head. He walked over to the corner where an old broom was leaning against the wall, and swept the cigarette butts and other trash into a pile.

Then he leaned against the front door and slid to the floor, looking around at the room. He pulled his phone out and started making a list. He needed paint supplies, cleaning supplies, and eventually furniture, but he decided to focus on just cleaning and painting for now. One step at a time.

CHAPTER 5

A Simple Three Card Spread

MAYA

Maya shuffled the cards and thought about what to do. She knew her family needed the old schoolhouse. She knew that it was the only place zoned for food service and the hotel wasn't making enough on its own. And she knew that this Tanner guy was in the way. *A simple three-card spread should do it*, she thought. She pulled the first card, representing the situation.

The Chariot, upright.

"No shit, Sherlock," Maya whispered to herself. The Chariot was a card of struggle and tension, the idea of someone being pulled in two directions. But it was also a card of action and willpower. It was about overcoming obstacles through determination to get what you want.

Well, if ever Maya was in a situation where she needed to overcome obstacles through determination, now was it.

Maya pulled the second card, the one representing the obstacle, and laid it across the first. The Knight of Swords.

Huh, Maya thought. The Knight of Swords was about change and chaos. Something coming into your life that turned everything upside down. Maya knew it could also sometimes represent an actual person coming into your life to turn everything upside down, and she frowned in annoyance. Fucking Tanner Sullivan. Either way, the meaning of the card was clear to her. The Clarks were supposed to get the old schoolhouse, and Tanner had come and fucked it up.

Finally, Maya pulled the final card, the one representing advice.

The Tower.

"Why am I always pulling The Tower lately?" Maya grumbled. It was such a violent-looking card. The image of a tall building with flames coming out of the upper windows, people jumping into the stormy waters below. Maya knew the card could have a positive meaning: "destroying the old to make way for the new," but did it always have to be this…disruptive?

Maya sat and gazed at the cards. It occurred to her that if she was a literal kind of person, and also possibly a psychopath, she would take the last card to mean that she should burn down the old schoolhouse so that no one could have it. But Maya was never one to interpret the cards literally. She used them more as a way of tuning in to her own subconscious. Some part of her usually already knew what to do in every situation—an oracle like a Tarot deck just helped her to see it.

Did The Tower mean she should destroy…Tanner? To make way for her family? That also felt psychotic. And it definitely didn't feel right to destroy her family to make room for Tanner. Maya didn't want to destroy anything or anyone. She just wanted her parents to be happy. She wanted her parents to have this thing they wanted so that…so that what?

She tried to envision telling her parents that she had gotten the old schoolhouse back. She pictured their eyes welling up, their smiles as they hugged her. That thought alone was enough. It would be worth it to get the building back just for that. But maybe it would even be enough to bridge that final gap she sometimes felt between her and her parents. Maybe she could, she didn't even know…take a few weeks off to go somewhere, maybe even pursue something else for a little while.

Because if she was being really truly completely honest with herself, she didn't love working for the hotel. She wasn't sure she wanted to do it for the rest of her life. Maybe if she could get the old schoolhouse so that her family could open a restaurant and solidify their finances, it would be enough for her to earn something for herself.

"Okay," she sighed. "So I guess I'm gonna try and get this Tanner guy to sell us the old schoolhouse."

Maya wasn't exactly sure how she was going to do this, but as soon as she said the words out loud, she felt a rush of certainty. She knew her parents had the money for it, and she knew they needed the money it would bring in.

Maya flopped back onto her bed and stared at the ceiling. She started to make a mental list of ways she could try and convince Tanner to let go of the building.

She didn't like any of them.

1. Talk to him.

Lay out the situation rationally, and provide him with other options for his coffee house or whatever the hell he was putting there. Which would involve, you know, talking to him. Which Maya did not want to do because she did not like him.

2. Seduce him.

If he fell madly in love with her, maybe she could get him to just give her the building. Which, okay, fine, might be like, 2% appealing. (Or maybe 10%?) But only because of the way he had held her arms so steadily earlier that morning when she bumped into him. His big, capable hands. And he had that good hair. And those hazel eyes. He was handsome. But, Maya reminded herself, he was also probably a raging misogynist, so even if she did manage to seduce him, he might not listen to a word she said. Plus, she didn't even know if he was single.

3. Blackmail.

Find some deep dark secret from his past and threaten to reveal it to the world unless he gave up the old schoolhouse. Which involved a level of deceit that Maya didn't feel totally comfortable with. She realized that she was probably capable of it, and that made her even more uncomfortable.

4. Threats?

That felt a bit too much like blackmail. Plus, Maya didn't really know what she could threaten him with.

5. Witchcraft.

Maya knew that there were plenty of witches who hexed and charmed their way through life, casting spells to make people do what they wanted them to. But that wasn't quite part of Maya's belief system. Both metaphysically, and ethically. There was a difference between casting a spell with a prayer to get laid, and slipping someone a love potion to make them have sex with you. Maya was the kind of witch who did the former, not the latter.

Maya sighed. Of all of her options, the first one seemed like the best one. Probably the only one, actually. She sat up and grabbed her phone and keys and headed out the door to Anne's house.

ANNE FROWNED as Maya told her what had happened in

the bar. "He glared at you?" she asked. "This guy just glared at you after the creep wouldn't leave you alone?"

"A full-on glare," Maya replied. "Or at least, like, a really deep frown." She bounced baby Tommy on her lap, where he was happily chewing on one of her bracelets.

Anne looked out into the woods from her seat on the porch, where she and Maya were sitting. "That just seems…weird," she finally said.

"Weird and gross and misogynistic, you mean?"

"Well, yeah."

"That is not even the main part of this story," Maya said. She told Anne about going with her family to the real estate office that morning, and about how Ruby told them that the old schoolhouse was already sold and that it had been sold to the *very same jerk from the bar the night before.* "Apparently his name is Tanner Sullivan, and he wants to turn the old schoolhouse into a coffee shop, and if he succeeds, we will never go there ever," Maya finished.

"Woof," Anne said.

"Yeah. Woof."

The two women were silent for a while, Tommy's gurgles the only sound aside from the birdsong around them.

"So, what are you going to do?" Anne asked.

"I want to try and get the old schoolhouse back."

"And how are you going to do that?"

Maya sighed. "I thought about threatening or blackmailing him, hexing him, or seducing him, but I think I'll probably have to just talk to him." She turned baby Tommy and held him so that he was facing her, his little legs sturdy on her lap as he pushed himself to standing. "Auntie Maya's going to be a good person and not do anything illegal," she cooed to him. He responded by patting her cheeks with his sticky hands. The front of his onesie was already soaked with drool.

Maya looked at Anne. "If this was any other baby," she said, "I would hand him back immediately because this is disgusting."

Anne laughed. "I can take him if you want."

"No, I love him the most," Maya said, squeezing the baby to her. She turned to cover his little cheek and neck with kisses, making him giggle, which was the best sound in the whole entire world.

"Would you make up your mind about how you feel about my baby?" Anne laughed.

"I can't help it. I'm a Gemini," Maya replied.

"Did I tell you he's got a tooth coming in?!" Anne said. "That's why he's drooling like a madman."

Maya looked at Tommy with awed excitement. "You gots a tooth? You'll be able to devour human flesh soon!"

"He kind of already does," Anne replied, rubbing one of her breasts. "My nipples are a…wasteland."

Maya laughed. "That sounds horrible."

"It is. It's how I discovered that he grew a tooth."

"Well, if it's for a new tooth, I can forgive him for covering my wrist and face and shoulder with drool."

The two women watched Tommy as he babbled and gestured. It was still astonishing to Maya that this baby existed. That her best friend had grown an entire human. It made her feel like they were actual adults. She'd had the sense that she had been masquerading for the past few years. But now they were the ones sitting on porches with babies, instead of their parents.

"What was this guy's name again?" Anne asked.

"The asshole from the bar?"

"Don't say 'asshole' in front of the baby!"

"Sorry, the fuckface from the bar?"

Anne laughed. "Yes."

"Tanner Sullivan."

"So you're going to talk to Tanner Sullivan and try to convince him to give up the old schoolhouse so that your family can buy it instead."

"Yep," Maya said. "I know for a fact there are other spaces in town where he could build his stupid coffee shop. Ruby literally said there were places zoned for food service that could be cafes."

"And your family can't do a cafe?"

Maya shook her head. "It needs to be able to serve more people to be worth it. So I refuse to let Tanner keep the old schoolhouse."

"Especially since it means you'd have to see him all the time."

Maya stared at Anne blankly for a moment before saying, "Oh shit, I didn't even think of that."

Maya imagined the years ahead of her if she didn't succeed in getting the old schoolhouse back. She hadn't realized that it would mean this asshole would be practically on their property for the rest of the foreseeable future. She'd have to dodge him at all hours. Customers would ask if the coffee shop next door was any good, and she'd be reminded over and over again of the catastrophe. At least she could have the satisfaction of telling them the coffee was horrible and the man who ran it was worse, but it wasn't much consolation.

"I really need to convince him," Maya said.

"What are you going to say to him?"

"I'm still deciding. Part of me thinks it would easier to seduce him."

Anne raised her eyebrows. "Do you...want to seduce him?"

Maya felt her stomach drop slightly at the thought. She

remembered the feeling of his hands on her arms again, their gentle but capable grip, those hazel eyes peering down at her. She'd have to stand on her tiptoes if she wanted to kiss him. Even then, she might not be tall enough. He'd have to crouch down, his hips flush against her, his arms wrapping tightly around her as their lips met. Maya wondered if his beard would be soft or rough against her skin, if he was the kind of man who would brush her hair out of her face to kiss her.

"Maya?"

Anne's voice snapped Maya out of her thoughts. "Huh?"

"I asked if you wanted to seduce Tanner Sullivan."

"No, I do not," Maya replied.

CHAPTER 6

We'll Do This The Hard Way

TANNER

Tanner was at the old schoolhouse by eight o'clock in the morning. He'd been getting there at the same time every day for a week, ever since he bought the building. He spent his days scrubbing down the hardwood floors, filling holes in the walls, cleaning the windows. It was the kind of quiet, steady work he enjoyed. Hell, it was the only kind of work he knew how to do. He'd never gone to college, and at age 28, he had roughly ten years of construction work experience on his resume, and not much else.

But that was all right with him. It wasn't just that construction was something he fell into—he genuinely enjoyed it. He liked working with his hands. He liked making something where there had been nothing, or taking something old and crumbling and making it new.

Tanner was bad at a lot of things, but construction wasn't one of them. As Tanner gathered his tools for the day, he thought gratefully about how easily construction came to him. It was just about the only thing that had. He really considered himself good at only two things: construction and speaking up for himself.

Construction just felt natural. Speaking up for himself had taken practice. It had started with the biggest, knock-down, drag-out fight he and his dad had ever had, right after Billy had gotten arrested. By the end of that night, after both of them had hit each other, Tanner had told Len that he was done.

When he had stomped down the stairs, his teeth bloody and his head ringing, he told himself that he'd never again take shit from anybody. It was the last time he'd ever talked to Len. From that moment on, he'd been determined to speak up for himself, to tell people what he wanted or needed, to take up space. (And at six foot five, he couldn't help but take up space.) It hadn't been easy, but he felt good about what the last few years had looked like.

Mostly.

There was Camille. And he cared a lot about her. Things were good. Except that she still wouldn't call him her boyfriend, even though that's absolutely what he was. He had been for a year now. It was their one ongoing fight —him asking her to just…claim him as her own. To say the words "This is my boyfriend, Tanner." Whenever she introduced him to someone new, she would just say "This is Tanner." It's true that she *acted* like a girlfriend, and wasn't afraid to hold hands or kiss in public, or share couple-y selfies. They weren't seeing other people. So Tanner tried not to let it bother him that she wouldn't call him her boyfriend. At least Tanner was still standing up for himself there, telling Camille what he wanted.

By ten o'clock, Tanner was sweating, his flannel in a heap on the floor. Even though the nights were still cold in May, the days were getting warmer. He had taken a break from taping the baseboards and was standing in his white work t-shirt and jeans, arms folded, looking up at the ceiling beams when he heard a knock at the door.

Tanner frowned. He didn't know a single person in town—even the fishermen from that night at the bar were only there for a few days.

Another knock. Tanner turned and walked towards the door. When he opened it, he was temporarily stunned. It was the girl from the bar. (And from the real estate office, now.) Her long hair laid in waves over her shoulders, and good hell, she had a jawline that looked like it had been chiseled out of marble. All of her could have been chiseled out of marble. He resisted the urge to look her up and down. He'd been wondering about her for days and now she was standing there at the door, looking at him.

Or uh, glaring at him? Her arms were folded across her chest and she was practically tapping one toe with impatience.

"Hi," Tanner finally managed.

"Can I come in?" the woman said. She didn't wait for an answer, but shoved past him into the building.

"Yes?" Tanner said.

The woman walked to the center of the room, then spun around and faced him. Tanner's breath practically caught. Her gaze was fixed and steady, and it was…well, it was hot as hell.

"Listen," she said, after staring at him for a few moments. "I'm going to get right to the point. My family has been planning on buying this building for months, maybe even years, and I came here to ask you to sell it to us."

Tanner couldn't quite figure out what to say. He was still processing her presence, and her request was a little too much for him to comprehend right away. He stood by the open door and looked at the woman, and when he finally spoke, it was a question.

"What's your name?"

The woman raised her eyebrows. "Maya Clark," she finally said. "And you're Tanner Sullivan."

Tanner raised his eyebrows in return. He was finding his footing in this conversation, even if it had taken him a moment. "Okay, Maya Clark," he said. "Nice to meet you." When Maya didn't shake his outstretched hand, he reached his other hand up and said, "Fine, I'll shake my own hand." He could have sworn he saw Maya's lips quirk, but she soon replaced the expression with a stony glare. He backed up and leaned against the wall near the front door. "Why does your family want to buy the building?" he asked.

"Why does it matter?"

Tanner shrugged. "I bought the building, fair and square, and if I'm going to give it up, I should know what I'm giving it up for."

Maya narrowed her eyes at him. "When were you born?" she asked.

"October 19th, 1993," Tanner replied, eyebrows raised.

"What *time* were you born?"

"No idea," he said. After a beat, he added, "Is that relevant to why your family wants to buy the building?"

"My family wants to buy the building to turn it into a restaurant connected to our hotel."

Tanner looked at Maya. It was very inconvenient how attractive she was. He changed the subject.

"Where's your family's hotel?"

Maya pointed out the window at the stucco building across the street. It was a small operation, two stories, all the rooms facing the parking lot. The sign out front said "The Hitchin' Post Hotel." Tanner had gotten used to the sight, passing it on his way to walk past the old school-house. It struck him as surprising that the woman he had been thinking about for days had been right there the whole time.

Maya folded her arms again. "My parents bought it three decades ago, and they've invested and renovated and expanded it every year since. And now they want this building to build a restaurant."

Tanner thought for a moment. "Why not build the restaurant somewhere else?"

"Nowhere else is big enough and zoned for food service." She paused. "We'll pay you whatever you paid for it. Maybe even more."

Tanner looked at the ground for a long time, his thoughts churning. He wished Maya had asked him for something else, because he loved the idea of giving her what she wanted. It was just that he couldn't give her this. "I can't sell you the building," he finally said.

It took Maya a moment to answer. "Why not?" she demanded.

He looked up at her. "Because. It's important to me."

"Yeah, well, it's important to me, too," Maya replied angrily.

The two of them looked at one another. Tanner had the sense of a stand-off, both of them standing with their arms folded, waiting for the other one to say something. Maya was attractive even when she was angry. Tanner wanted to walk over to her and run his thumb over her full lips until her frown was gone, and then—

She was walking towards him. Her purposeful stride made something warm and hungry awaken in his chest, and he swallowed hard. At the last moment, she breezed past him and pushed open the door.

"Fine," she said. "We'll do this the hard way." And then she was gone.

Tanner stared at the door, then glanced out of the window to watch Maya walk across the street and towards the hotel.

We'll do this the hard way? he thought. That sounded… ominous. He couldn't imagine what she meant by it. He did feel a little guilty about the old schoolhouse now. Maya's family must have felt like he'd snatched it out from right under their noses. But then he thought back to that rainy afternoon with his mom and Billy when he was a teenager, and he knew he couldn't buy any other space. This was the one he wanted. And even though it sounded a little childish, he'd gotten here first. In his mind, emotional attachment trumped convenience of location.

Maybe he could work out some sort of deal with the hotel. Give his customers 10% off at the hotel, and they could have coupons for the cafe or something. He tumbled the idea around in his head while he went back to his task of taping the baseboards. Three cans of deep blue paint sat in the middle of the room, ready to be spread onto the walls.

Maya. Maya Clark. Maya Clark with the confident walk and strong jawline and silky brown hair and the body that wouldn't quit. He realized he had never seen her give a genuine smile, but he suspected that if he ever did, he'd be done for. Her lips were full and pillowy, and he could imagine pressing his mouth to them…

Snap out of it, Tanner told himself.

His phone rang.

"This is a collect call from an inmate at California State Prison Solano. To accept this call, press one."

"Hey, Billy," Tanner said.

"Did you get the place?"

"Yeah. I'm here right now."

"Hell yes! What's it like?"

Tanner looked around, the floors cleaned, the walls patched, the baseboards partway taped.

"It's good," he said. "It'll be a helluva lot more work to turn it into an actual coffee house, but I've spent the last while cleaning and repairing stuff, and it's gonna be good."

"Dude, I'm so pumped for you," Billy said.

"Thanks," Tanner said, smiling. "You know you're working here when you get out, right?"

"I would have burned the place down if you hadn't offered me a job."

Tanner shook his head. "Don't say shit like that."

"I've already done aggravated assault, why not add arson to my record?"

"I'm gonna go," Tanner said.

"Okay, fuck you, then," Billy said affectionately.

"Fuck you, too."

For the third time, Tanner got back to taping down baseboards, trying not to think too hard about Maya Clark.

CHAPTER 7

Horoscopes & Soaps

MAYA

Maya had not been prepared for Tanner Sullivan's voice. She was also still not used to how big he was, like he'd just been scaled up somehow, but she'd at least been prepared for it. She hadn't gotten a full sense of his voice when he was talking in the crowded bar, but standing in the old schoolhouse with him just now, she had discovered that his voice was…powerful.

It was warm and low and rumbly, like if molasses or mahogany had a sound. Or if a dark whiskey was also somehow a thick flannel blanket? Maya was having trouble forming coherent thoughts about it. She stomped upstairs to her room and flung herself onto her bed.

"'We'll do this the hard way'?!" she repeated to herself. That's what she had left Tanner with. What the hell did she even mean? It sounded impressively bad-ass and kind of threatening, but the reality was that Maya had no idea what to do next. She had hoped that in talking to him, the solution would just sort of present itself. That she'd navigate the conversation in such a way that she would be inspired to know exactly the right thing to say to convince him to sell her family the property. That had...not happened.

Instead she'd asked him what his astrological sign was, and then made a very vague threat before leaving.

She pulled her phone out. "October 19, 1993," she whispered. He was *clearly* a Libra, with all of his holding on to the old schoolhouse because he bought it fair and square, and defending it with such casualness. He had all of that laidback charisma that Libras have. Plus, he avoided conflict by just...dismissing it? She opened up one of her horoscope apps and entered Tanner's date of birth in.

"Libra sun, Capricorn moon," she said to herself. She scrolled through the app a bit more before tossing her phone aside. "Well, that's annoying."

Maya didn't know many Capricorns, but according to her app, they were patient and hardworking and mature. Which Maya found...attractive. So *fine*, maybe she found Tanner Sullivan attractive. That didn't mean she had to do anything about it.

Maya laid on her bed, staring at the ceiling, debating with herself for a few minutes. Finally, she sat up enough to grab her phone again. Then she typed in "Libra and Gemini compatibility," and read what the app had to say.

Geminis and Libras make great partners, since they're both air signs. Both tend to be outgoing, curious, and laidback in their relation- ships, which works great in any romance. Their playful sides make the beginning of their love story fun and flirtatious, with plenty of great chemistry.

When it comes to sex, this couple tends to have fun, fulfilling experiences. When a Gemini's "down-for-anything" attitude meets a Libra's desire for balance, mutual satisfaction is all but guaranteed.

Maya pursed her lips. If "great chemistry" meant "strong dislike," then the app had it right. As for the "mutual satisfaction"…well, Maya decided not to think about that.

Since her conversation with Tanner hadn't magically created any solutions, Maya tried to figure out what "doing this the hard way" actually meant, if anything at all. But her mind kept tumbling the same thoughts over and over again: talking to Tanner hadn't worked, and also Tanner was annoyingly attractive. Her brain kept hitting dead ends.

Maya sighed. She could always think better when she was doing something with her hands. She walked over to the corner of the kitchen where she kept all of her Tindale Soap Co. supplies—oil, soap base, scents, packaging supplies, and dozens of other items crammed into one small corner of chaos. She pulled up her spreadsheet of inventory and made a list of things to make more of.

When Maya was a teenager, Anne's mom, Debbie, had taught her how to make soap, and she'd spent years doing it as a hobby. A few years ago, she had the idea of offering the soap to guests at the hotel, and then she expanded into lotions and lip balms. She sold it to her family at a discount, and they got a local handmade product to brag to the hotel guests about.

Then Debbie heard about it, and then Dr. Zhao, and then Jamie at the fly-fishing shop, and then all of them started making requests for orders of their own. Not to sell —just to have for themselves.

At this point, Maya was basically running a small business with a dozen clients. She didn't make a ton of money at it, but she had a logo and branded packaging, and she was proud of how far she'd come. And it was something she enjoyed doing. There was something relaxing about stirring soap mixtures, adding scents and colors, cutting and packaging the bars.

Maya gathered the ingredients and started melting down soap base.

She secretly wanted to use fun (absurd) names for her soaps, but because her main clientele were hotel guests, she stuck to generic, descriptive names. But she had a mental list of what she would call each soap if she could do things her own way. She and Anne and their friend Cosimo had come up with a bunch of names late one night when they were helping her with orders:

Citrus Sunrise would be "Orange You Glad To Be Clean" (Cosimo).

Apple Awake would be "Ugh Everyone Is Obsessed With Fall" (Anne).

Pine Forest would be "She Pined in Thought" (Anne's suggestion, from Shakespeare) or "Literally Just Tindale Park" (Maya).

Honey Oatmeal would be "Breakfast Bath" (Cosimo).

Eucalyptus Soother would be "Eucalyp-dis DICK," which might not be great from a marketing perspective, but Maya had come up with it and thought it was too funny to not use.

It was something Maya still did—brainstorm new soap scents and designs, and coming up with her own spin on what to call it. As she stirred in the scents for her Teak Mahogany soap ("In the Teaky Teaky Teaky Teaky Teaky Room"), she had a brief vision of doing this full-time, instead of working at the hotel.

She imagined having more than just one corner of her family's kitchen. (She'd asked for more space once, but her request had been quickly dismissed.) She pictured a little shop somewhere in West Tindale—a window display of candles and soaps and lotions, mason jars and wood crates and all the things tourists went nuts for. Maybe she could start a Soap-of-the-Month club, where people could sign up to get a small sample of a new soap scent every month. Her orders already almost ran on a subscription service, they were so regular. She'd change all the packaging to reflect the names she wanted to give each soap. Run sales, hold giveaways, get an Instagram.

Maya sighed as she stirred. Unless she could quit the hotel, none of this was possible. There just wasn't time. Or at least there wasn't time to work at the hotel, expand the soap business, and have her sanity. It was never something she thought about seriously. Just a little daydream to keep her from going stir-crazy.

Besides, she was a Clark. Clarks were loyal to the Clarks, and Bruce and Harriett Clark had poured decades of work into their family business, so it only made sense to keep the business in the family.

And leaving it didn't really seem like an option. She thought briefly about her uncle Conrad, who had been there at the beginning of the Hitchin' Post Hotel, before Maya and Devan were born. Bruce, Harriett, and had started the hotel together, but when Conrad left the business, it had caused a big falling out.

She'd asked about it once, when she was a teenager. But her parents refused to give her any details. She still had never met her uncle Conrad. Her dad rarely talked about him.

After the soap had been scented and poured into molds, Maya began packaging up orders to distribute that evening. She always loved walking the one square mile of town, handing out paper bags or cardboard boxes full of soaps and lotions and lip balms. Sometimes she thought about her time in Boston, going to school, living in a big city. It had been such a welcome change from living at home with her parents. But when it came down to it, it wasn't the small town of West Tindale that bothered her, really. Silver Falls wasn't too far away if she needed a little culture, and in the busy season, the town was full of enough tourists to meet her needs, both socially and romantically.

Maya glanced at the clock, then bundled her packages into a tote bag. At the fly-fishing shop, Jamie waved Maya toward the till while he watched a baseball game on his ancient TV set. She took a twenty from the drawer and left two soaps and one lip balm on the counter.

"Hey, let me know if you want more lip balms for the shop," Maya said as she pocketed the twenty-dollar bill.

"Yeah, better get me some in the next few weeks if you can," Jamie said in his rough voice. "The season's started."

"You got it," Maya saluted, then headed out.

At Zhao's, she made half an attempt to decline the appetizers being offered to her, knowing the entire time that she was going to sit down and eat all of them. She chatted with the owner Joe, who asked for double his usual order of soaps next month. He wanted to send some to his children who lived out of town.

"You are going to have to quit the hotel and make soap full time," Joe said, smiling.

Maya returned his smile. "I wish," she replied. "The hotel comes before soap. But I'll make it work."

She stood and yelled a polite "thank you" to Mrs. Zhao in the kitchen, then grabbed her tote bag and headed out. She left a paper bag of soaps at the knife shop for Eli and his wife. She left another at the clinic, where Joe Zhao's son Mark asked about her family.

Maya took her time strolling through town to her last stop at Pages and Pasta. She walked past the hardware store and the Happy Bear Hotel (which *did* have a restaurant attached to their hotel, the fuckers). She turned at the

Happy Home Trailer Park, the usually vacant RV spots already starting to fill up for the summer.

The next block was filled with more shops, some of them more permanent than others. There was a t-shirt screen printing shop that had been there since her parents were young, and a jewelry store that had limped along through five summers. There was a small boutique that sold billowy scarves and tie-dyed pants.

At least there had been. Maya did a double-take at the window where the boutique had displayed its earth toned wares last year. But it was empty.

Maya pressed her face to the window. The shop was tiny—maybe eleven feet across and twenty feet deep. A few shelves sat empty along one wall, and one lone clothing rack stood forlornly in the middle of the room. There was a counter along the far wall, opposite the window.

Maya stepped back, then noticed the sign in the window. "For Lease." Ruby Broulette's name and phone number was listed beneath it. Maya frowned.

"Well, Tanner could fucking have *this* place," she said quietly. Although…

It was pretty small. It was hard to imagine cafe tables crowded into the room. And you'd have to use half the space for food prep anyways. So maybe this wouldn't be the best alternative for Tanner's stupid coffee shop.

A thought bubbled up in Maya's mind, which could then not be unthought.

This place could be a little soap shop. It would actually be a *perfect* little soap shop. Maya took a step back and looked at the storefront. She could picture the sign above the door. "Tindale Soap Co." Candles and soaps and lip balms in the window. A smile slowly crept across Maya's face.

She allowed herself one full minute of imagining

standing behind the counter in this little shop. Her own space, her own schedule, her own work. She would paint the walls sage green. No, a dusty rose. No, green.

Maya closed her eyes. Her own shop wasn't possible right now, not with the hotel demanding so much of her time. She sighed and kept walking towards Pages and Pasta.

CHAPTER 8

Belonging Somewhere

TANNER

Tanner thought about Maya's visit for the rest of the day. He had a girlfriend, so he alternated between thinking about Maya as a potential friend and trying not to think about her at all.

He was still feeling distracted at the end of the day, so instead of walking straight home that evening, Tanner decided to explore West Tindale. It meant going out of his way by several blocks, but the town was small enough that it didn't make too much of a difference. He started out down Pine Ridge Avenue, which, yes, did lead him right past Maya's family's hotel. Which he totally didn't do on purpose. He was happy to see the parking lot full.

Tanner walked onward, past the many shops that were bustling now that it was late May. The tourist season had officially and truly begun, and the streets were full—families, couples, college students from Silver Falls coming up for the weekend. There was a line of people outside the candy store, waiting to buy ice cream cones. Tanner thought back to that afternoon with his mom and Billy in the rainstorm, and a wave of missing them both washed over him.

Billy was only a phone call away—sort of. He definitely wasn't quite as reachable as he would be outside of prison. Tanner hoped that Billy could get an early release. He sent a silent prayer to whatever power was out there that Billy wouldn't get caught with his contraband cell phone.

He'd slowly gotten used to his mom's absence over the years. It was awful when she'd first died. Even though they'd known it was coming, it was still so incomprehensible that one day she was there and the next day she wasn't. For months, he kept forgetting, and losing her again in the remembering.

As Tanner walked, he slowly realized that one of the things he was feeling was just…loneliness. He was an introvert, and enjoyed spending most of his time alone. But it occurred to him that he didn't have friends here in West Tindale. Maya was really the only person he knew, if you could even count her. He'd left the other handful of people in his life back in Newcastle.

Was that part of why he was so drawn to Maya? Pure loneliness? Would he feel this way about anyone else close to his age whom he happened to run into on a regular basis?

Tanner thought about Maya's face, the way her eyes sparked when she looked at him.

Nah, he was pretty sure he felt a little bit more than friendliness toward Maya.

He should probably tamp that down, especially since Camille was coming for her first visit in two days.

He pulled out his phone. This time she answered on the second ring, and her face filled the screen.

"Hey, babe," Camille said. She gave him a warm smile, and relief flooded Tanner's chest.

"Hey," he said.

"I was actually about to call you."

"Yeah?" Tanner felt a smile stretch over his face.

"But I…um. It's kind of for a sucky reason. A court date got moved up."

"To when?"

"Three days from now. Tanner, I'm sorry, hon, but I can't make it out to West Tindale.

Tanner closed his eyes. He felt that familiar white-hot rage filling him up.

"Hey," Camille said softly. "Breathe."

Tanner wanted to punch a wall. He concentrated on inhaling slowly through his nose, and exhaling just as slowly through his mouth, until the feeling of anger passed. As soon as it was gone, it was replaced with self-loathing. He hated when he became this person. It was like a shadow of Len lived inside of him, taking over when something went wrong.

He wasn't even angry at Camille. He knew she didn't do it on purpose. Her clients couldn't control their court dates. He was frustrated by the circumstances. He'd been missing his girlfriend and now he had to wait even longer to see her.

"I'm sorry, Camille," he said.

"Hey," she replied. "You're okay. It's okay."

Tanner nodded. Camille's patience and compassion still took him by surprise. "I still haven't started remote therapy yet, but apparently I should."

Camille just smiled gently at him.

"And sorry you had to…you shouldn't have to calm me down," he added.

He heard a beep in the background. "Sorry, hon, I've got another call coming in from a client. Can I text you later?"

Tanner nodded, then watched her face blink away. He put his phone back in his pocket and sighed.

He'd have to figure out some kind of social life for when Camille wasn't here. (Which was apparently more now.) There was always the bar, even though he didn't drink. Maybe there were some…community events he could attend? Get himself involved in the town. If he remembered correctly, the bookstore usually had a community calendar. He turned and crossed to the other side of the street, making his way back up Pine Ridge towards "Pages and Pasta."

When he opened the door, the smell of warm bread greeted him. He closed his eyes and let it wash over him for a moment.

"I'll be with you in a minute!" A voice rang out.

Tanner looked around. On one side of the room, a small diner was set up, and on the other, a bookstore. It was like two separate businesses just sort of joined forces.

A man in a white shirt waved at him from behind the counter on the diner side. His brown hair was pulled back into a ponytail, and he wore a red-checked apron around his waist. "You want some food?" he asked.

Tanner hadn't planned on eating dinner here, but as soon as the man offered, he realized how hungry he was. "Sure," Tanner said.

"Have a seat anywhere."

Tanner glanced around, a handful of cafe tables spread along the wall near the windows. Most of them were full of couples and a few families, but he found one and sat down.

The man came out from the kitchen and leaned on the chair opposite Tanner. "What can I get you?"

Tanner looked around. He hadn't even glanced at the menu on the table. "Whatever's good," he said.

"Oh hey, I've seen you around town," the man suddenly said. "Are you here for the summer?"

"Yeah," Tanner said. "Just moved here from California."

"I'm Cosimo. My brother and I own this place with his wife and her mom."

Tanner reached up to shake Cosimo's outstretched hand. "Tanner," he said. "And yeah, I just bought the old schoolhouse."

Cosimo's eyes widened. "Oh, you're *that* Tanner," he said.

Tanner looked around. "Does West Tindale have like, a group chat or something?" he asked.

Cosimo laughed. "We're just a small community," he said. He clapped his hands once. "I'll bring you the special."

Cosimo walked back to the kitchen, and Tanner watched the families around him and the tourists walking past the window. He'd always loved West Tindale, and that love didn't change now that he lived here. In a few minutes, Cosimo set a plate of spaghetti bolognese in front of Tanner.

"Thanks," Tanner said. He took one bite and then he closed his eyes in ecstasy. It was the best food he'd had since moving to West Tindale. He ate slowly, watching the people walk by outside, thinking occasionally about the old schoolhouse, and the things he still had left to do. He was staring into space, his empty plate in front of him, when Cosimo stopped by.

"Can I get you anything else?" The man stood near the table, an armful of empty plates in his hands.

"No, man, this was great." Tanner said. Cosimo paused, then nodded.

A few minutes later, he showed up with a plate of tiramisu. "On the house," he said.

"You didn't have to do that," Tanner said.

Cosimo smiled. "You're new in town, yeah?"

Tanner nodded, and Cosimo answered with a shrug. "Food is…how to make friends," he said.

Tanner smiled, surprised. Hadn't he just been thinking about how lonely he was? He hesitated for a moment, then asked "Want to join me?" He felt awkward as hell, but he had to make friends somehow.

"I'm sure my boyfriend won't mind," Cosimo said, winking. He sat down in the chair opposite Tanner.

Tanner's stomach sank. "Oh, that's…sorry, I'm not…"

"Relax," Cosimo said with a quiet chuckle, pulling out an extra fork from his apron. "You're not my type." He reached over and cut into the tiramisu. "So did you grow up coming here?" he asked.

The two men sat for the next fifteen minutes, eating tiramisu and talking about where Tanner grew up, what he liked about West Tindale, what his plans were for the old schoolhouse coffee shop. They talked about Cosimo's family and the way the restaurant had evolved from the place his own late parents had started. Cosimo was easy to talk to.

And Tanner felt…at home. Like he could belong to something. Like he could belong here. In West Tindale, with these people. He'd spent his whole life trying to get away from home—home wasn't safe. And then, the only good things about home had been locked away in prison or taken by cancer. It was why he wanted to make Sullivan's a part of this community. He didn't want belonging just for the people in this town. He wanted it for himself.

The tables had slowly emptied around Tanner and Cosimo as they talked, the tiramisu long finished. Cosimo was in the middle of a story about his parents when the door opened behind them.

"Delivery!" a voice rang out. "I brought—"

The voice cut off, and Tanner turned around.

Maya stood just inside the door, a large tote bag over her shoulder. Tanner's breath caught. He didn't think he'd ever get over her stunning features. Her jawline was so… defined, sharp edges that disappeared under soft curtains of brown hair. Just now, her mouth was hanging open slightly as she took in the scene in front of her. But she quickly snapped her lips shut and looked away from Tanner.

"I brought more lip balm for the store," she said. "And soap for you and Debbie. I'll put it all in the back." Maya walked purposefully to a door near the counter. Tanner watched her go.

"Have you met Maya?" Cosimo asked.

Tanner snapped his eyes back to his new friend. "Kind of," he said.

A hint of a smile played around Cosimo's lips.

Tanner tried to keep the hopeful curiosity out of his voice. "Are you friends with her?" he asked.

Cosimo's smile widened. "We grew up together. And her best friend married my brother, so we're practically family at this point."

Tanner nodded. "You meant it when you said you're a small community."

Maya's voice interrupted his thoughts. "Careful, Cos," she said. Tanner looked over his shoulder at Maya as she walked out of the back room and approached their table. She leaned on Cosimo's chair and looked at Tanner. "This guy might take something you want right out from under you."

Tanner raised his eyebrows. "Are you calling me a thief?" he said.

"That's yet to be determined." Maya looked him up and down, and it heated something in his chest. And, frankly, in his pants. He resisted the need to shift in his seat.

"The only thing I steal is hearts," he said, then tried not to cringe. It was an okay line, but the delivery was…rough.

Maya's lips quirked up in a smile for half a second, and then she tamped it down.

"We'll have to see about that, too," she said. She pushed away from Cosimo's chair and then walked toward the door. "Bye, Cos! Love you!" Maya said sweetly. He watched her blow a kiss to Cosimo and give them both a stunning smile before she stepped outside. Tanner felt slightly dazed as he turned back around.

"Love you," Cosimo said after waving to Maya. He turned back to Tanner and looked like he was about to say something, but he shut his mouth in a small smile instead.

Tanner and Cosimo exchanged phone numbers before he left, and he walked out of the store feeling a little lighter. He had at least one friend in West Tindale, and he carried the hope of it with him through the rest of his walk home.

Maybe he could really, finally belong somewhere.

CHAPTER 9
Carte Blanche
MAYA

Later that evening, Harriet intercepted Maya as she was headed up the stairs.

"Maya, honey," she said, laying a hand on her daughter's arm.

"Yeah?"

"Could you come here a minute? Your dad and I wanted to talk to you about something."

Maya's stomach clenched. Those words were usually followed by some sort of…reckoning. Something she'd forgotten to do or not done well enough, or some other way that she'd disappointed her parents. But there was no avoiding the conversation, whatever it was about. Putting it off would only make it worse.

"Sure," Maya said, following her mom to the largest bedroom at the end of the hall. It always made Maya feel like a teenager again, walking down the seemingly endless hallway, feeling like she was heading towards the executioner.

Bruce was sitting on the bed, his reading glasses on, his

laptop on his knees. He looked up when Maya and Harriet entered the room.

"Hey, Sweetie," he said, closing the laptop. "Have a seat." Maya perched on the edge of the bed, while her mother went around to the other side of the bed and sat down beside Bruce.

"We've been thinking," Bruce began, "about the old schoolhouse. We know we were too late to buy the old schoolhouse, but we really want to give it one more go." He paused to glance at his wife. "To be transparent, we're not sure if we can stay afloat much longer without an additional revenue stream. We were wondering if you'd be willing to go talk to this Tanner fellow, see if you can convince him to sell it to us."

Maya was quiet. She didn't tell her parents that she had already tried (and failed) to do what they were asking.

"Why me?" she finally asked. "Why don't you ask him?"

Bruce and Harriet looked at each other for a brief moment, then Harriet answered in a low voice. "We think it would be better coming from someone closer to his own age. He might listen better to you or Devan, but Devan is…well, you know Devan."

Maya nodded. She loved her brother, but he could be quick to speak before thinking.

"We're also giving you this," Bruce said, handing over a small piece of paper.

Maya took it and then looked up. "A blank check?" she asked.

"Offer him what you can," Harriet said. "Start low, obviously, but anything up to $200,000."

Maya's eyebrows shot up. "You're just giving me a blank check to try and convince Tanner Sullivan to sell us the old schoolhouse."

Harriet spoke. "We're also…well, honey, you're a grown woman. And that's the other reason we think it should be you and not Devan. Consider this a blank check in more ways than one. A true 'carte blanche,' if you will."

If Maya's eyebrows could have raised any higher, they would have flown off her face. She wasn't entirely sure how to interpret what her parents were telling her, but it sounded an awful lot like "do whatever you have to do." With maybe a hint of "use your feminine wiles to get what you want"?

She looked down at the check, thinking. "Up to $200,000?" she said.

When she looked back up at her parents, they were both smiling. Bruce reached out and laid his hand over hers. "We knew you could do this for us, sweetie," he said.

"We believe in you," Harriet added, a little too enthusiastically.

Maya nodded, then stood up. "Anything else?" she asked.

"There's no rush," Bruce said. "But if you could try and talk to him in the next two weeks?"

Maya nodded again. "Next two weeks, up to $200,000, carte blanche. Got it." She turned and left her parents' room and walked down the hall to collapse in her own bed. She pulled out her phone and texted Anne.

> I think my parents just implied that I should seduce Tanner Sullivan into selling us the old schoolhouse.

> Did they use the word "seduce"?

> No, but they did use the phrase "carte blanche" in the same sentence as "you're a grown woman" so

Uhhhh

I know it's late, but do you mind if I come over?

As long as you know that I might fall asleep partway through hanging out, then yes. Just come in when you get here. Tommy's already asleep.

When Maya got to the cabin and pushed open the front door, she found Anne curled up in a blanket in front of the wood stove, reading a book. Roberto was in the kitchen washing dishes. Anne looked up, and Maya smiled at the scene. When they were all in high school, Maya didn't spend a lot of time thinking about their futures. But if anyone had asked her what she pictured, it would probably be something like this.

"Hey," Roberto said quietly, looking up from the sink.

"Hey," Maya replied softly. "Are we whispering? What's happening?"

"Roberto just barely got Tommy back down," Anne said quietly, leaning over to put her book down, then patting the spot next to her on the couch.

Maya walked over and settled in. "I thought he was already asleep when you texted me?"

Anne sighed. "Apparently babies don't like sleeping when they have teeth coming in. It's a whole thing."

"I mean, if I were pushing bones out of the flesh of my mouth, I probably wouldn't sleep great either."

"Fair," Anne said. "Okay, tell me what the hell your parents actually said." She glanced over at Roberto, then at Maya again. "Unless this is a private conversation."

"I can barely hear you anyway," Roberto said.

"Then how did you hear us well enough to comment on it?" Maya asked, turning to him.

"Fine, I'll go upstairs," he said, rolling his eyes good-naturedly.

"I mean, you can tell Roberto any of this," Maya said. "At this point in the…saga."

Anne raised her eyebrows. "It's a saga?"

"Okay, so I tried talking to Tanner this afternoon," Maya began, but Anne punched her lightly in the arm.

"Why didn't you lead with that?!"

"I am!"

"I meant in your text," Anne said.

"Well, I'm leading with it now. So I went over to the old schoolhouse and tried to talk Tanner into selling us the building, but it was a no go. He just stood there in his stupid tank top with his shoulders and his jeans or whatever and looked at me with his hazel eyes and said the building was important to him and that he wouldn't sell it."

By the end of Maya's speech, a hint of a smile was playing around Anne's lips.

"What?" Maya asked.

Anne lowered her voice an octave and said, "If I didn't know any better, Belle, I'd think you had feelings for this beast."

Maya laughed. "Okay, the actual line is 'feelings for this *monster*,' and also never quote a Disney movie at me in this context again."

"How am I not supposed to quote the Disney movie at you when you knew the line so well you needed to correct me on it?!"

"You can quote Disney movies at me, but not when you're accusing me of having feelings for a stranger."

"You didn't deny it, though," Anne said, grinning.

"Because there's nothing to deny."

Anne sat up. "So you don't deny it?!"

Maya leaned back and stared at the ceiling with an exaggerated moan. "That's not what I meeeaaaaaant."

"Okay fine," Anne said. "So tell me what happened with your parents."

When Maya finished telling Anne what her parents had said, Anne turned and looked into the fire. "I don't know," she said slowly. "It could kind of go either way. Like, that they were hinting that you should seduce him, or that they just were giving you power to negotiate the price." She was quiet for a few moments. "Do you want to seduce him?"

"We've already talked about this," Maya said.

"*Have* we actually talked about this? You seducing Tanner?"

"I said I didn't want to, and that's all the talking we need to do," Maya said. She took a deep breath. "The point is that my parents gave me an actual physical blank check and told me to get the old schoolhouse from Tanner, and that we desperately need the restaurant to stay afloat, so that's what I'm going to do."

CHAPTER 10

Talks With Billy

TANNER

Okay, so Tanner had already admitted to himself that he found Maya attractive. That was just an…objective observation. Any stranger could see she was stunning. So he couldn't figure out why he kept thinking about her. In decidedly…not platonic ways.

Tanner could picture Maya on every surface in every room of his house. Even though, to be honest, there weren't that many surfaces. Mostly the floor and the mattress on the floor. And his kitchen counters. Maybe this was the real motivation for getting a table and chairs. So he could picture bending Maya over them.

Or uh…Camille. That's who he should be picturing. His girlfriend.

He was trying to not let his brain go too haywire, but Maya was like some sort of lust ghost that haunted his apartment. He kept thinking of the way she looked at him that day when she came into the old schoolhouse and said that thing about doing things the hard way, and then the way she looked at him again at Pages and Pasta. And the more he thought about it, the more she was driving him crazy.

He had dealt with it first by calling Camille, which didn't work because she didn't answer, and then by throwing himself into the renovation. He ordered tables and chairs for the coffee shop, and finally gave in and ordered a couch as well. He was worried about people spilling on it, but if he wanted the place to be cozy and inviting, a couch made the most sense. And he could buy a cover for it if he had to.

On Friday afternoon, while he was at the old schoolhouse, measuring the room to prepare for building a counter, his phone rang. He glanced at the screen, then swiped to answer. An automated voice spoke.

"This is a collect call from an inmate at California State Prison Solano. To accept this call, press one."

After Tanner pressed one, Billy didn't even wait to greet his brother, but just started swearing.

"Hey, man," Tanner said, immediately trying to keep his voice calm. Billy let out another string of curse words.

Tanner set his measuring tape down and sat cross-legged on the floor. "Billy?"

Billy hadn't stopped talking since Tanner answered the phone. "Everything is so fucked, like, you try and none of these fuckers give a shit about you—"

"Billy!" Tanner tried one more time to get Billy's attention before realizing that Billy just needed to yell for a minute. So he let Billy rant, trying to concentrate on keeping his own breathing slow and even. He could feel his jaw clenching, so he kept reminding himself to relax. He had a hard time following Billy's rant, but eventually he got that one of the CO's had cut off Billy's time with the weights, for no reason (in Billy's mind). Tanner had no idea if Billy had done something to deserve this consequence, but it didn't actually matter. Either way, Billy was still furious.

After a few minutes, Tanner finally said, "Billy. Take a deep breath. Breathe with me for a minute."

Billy slowed his tirade down enough to take a few deep breaths, even if some of them included growls of frustration. Tanner said, "Okay. Do the color thing."

"There are no goddamn colors in here, man," Billy said, his voice ramping up again.

"Just name two, then," Tanner replied. "Just name two colors you can see."

"Beige and beige."

Tanner couldn't help but smile. "I guess that counts." Billy had been to multiple therapists over the years, and to more than one juvenile detention center. He had learned the color trick from a therapist when he was fourteen or so, and Tanner used it whenever Billy seemed to be getting too close to the ledge of his anger.

"Fuck these COs, man," Billy said.

"Fuck 'em," Tanner agreed. He knew a CO or two was probably listening in on their conversation, but it seemed worth the risk to help Billy feel better.

"It makes me want to…I dunno, man. I feel like I could punch through walls right now."

Tanner ran his finger over the scar on his hand. "I don't recommend it," he said.

"I know. They're cement or whatever in here, anyway."

It was silent for a moment, the two brothers breathing in sync, the background noise of the prison on Billy's end of the line.

"I hate this feeling, man," Billy finally said. "Like…red rage just coming down."

Tanner nodded. He wondered if there was something

genetic about it, if Len had passed it on to his two sons. Tanner felt like that same rage constantly lived inside him, and while it slept most of the time, sometimes he felt it reach up to the surface to remind him of who he was and who he came from.

"I know," he said out loud. He paused. "Are you doing okay now?"

"Yeah," Billy said, although his voice was still tight. "I'm trying to keep it together in here, but it's rough, man."

"I know," Tanner said, then paused. "Well, I guess I don't know. But the judge said you could petition for early release in September. That's only a few months away. Just keep your cool until then."

"I'm trying, man."

"I know you are."

Another silence.

"Dude," Billy said. "There's a class in here where they had us do that vision board thing that I did in juvey. Do you remember that?"

"Hell yes," Tanner said. "That thing changed my life and I wasn't even the one in juvey."

Billy laughed, and Tanner felt the sound of it relax his shoulders a little bit more. He knew Billy's temper was quick to flare up, but it could cool down fairly quickly as well.

"I straight up forgot about that shit," Billy said. "The thing was insane, dude. I had all kinds of crazy shit on there. A jet-ski, an Apple Watch, dating Beyoncé."

It was Tanner's turn to laugh.

"They said to put anything you wanted," Billy continued, "Even if it was totally impossible, but I was really swinging for the fences, man."

"You never know," Tanner replied. "I bet Jay-Z never

thought he'd be dating Beyoncé. There's still time for you, man."

"Ha ha," Billy said dryly. "Anyway, they had us do a vision board and then make a list of stuff we wanted when we got out."

"Like a Christmas list?"

Billy huffed out a surprised laugh. "Yeah, like a Christmas list. But it felt good, you know? Just writing it down." Tanner waited for his brother to share more about the list, but the two brothers sat in silence for a few moments instead. Billy was the one to break it. "Hey man, I gotta go. Thanks for talking me down."

"Anytime," Tanner said.

"Bye."

Tanner sighed as he put his phone away. He never said it out loud, but there was a part of him that hated how much he and Billy were alike. Sometimes when Billy got angry, it was like looking in a mirror. Tanner liked to think he could control his temper, but Billy had always used his fists first and his words second. Tanner wondered if one day, he himself would snap…if something would set him off and he'd be swinging before he even knew what was happening. The thought scared the shit out of him. He didn't want to be Billy. He didn't want to be his dad.

So instead he named colors and he took deep breaths and was quiet when he needed to be. Camille was always trying to get him to "open up." He didn't know how to explain to her that he was afraid of what would come out if he did.

Tanner stood up and finished measuring the space, writing notes in his notebook. He glanced over at the boxes of curtains and curtain rods along one wall, then glanced at the time. He was trying to keep a semi-regular work schedule, but he also knew that he could do whatever the hell he wanted, since he was his own boss now. He smiled at the thought, then pulled out the ladder to begin mounting the curtain rods.

The old schoolhouse had a lot of windows, and they were tall. There were windows on three of the four walls, all of them except the back wall, the one towards the woods. Tanner had debated about blinds or curtains, but curtains seemed cozier. He had purchased some that went practically ceiling to floor, in a rich mustardy yellow fabric, thick enough to block out the light. Tanner didn't know much about design, but he liked the way the yellow looked against the deep blue of the walls.

Tanner climbed the ladder on the south wall, a handful of tools in his hands and pockets, and glanced out the side window. The Hitchin' Post Hotel was right across the street, and Tanner paused as he looked at it.

There was a significant part of him that did feel guilty about taking this building from Maya's family. But he couldn't see any way around the reality that he also wanted the old schoolhouse, and that he was building something he hoped would be meaningful out of it.

As he climbed back down the ladder to grab a few screws and his drill, he caught movement outside. He paused and watched as a figure hurried away from the front office door and hid around the corner, leaning against the wall that faced him. It didn't take Tanner long to recognize Maya. Something in his chest leapt at the sight of her. He watched as she glanced around, then pulled a few things out of her pocket.

He smiled. He wasn't 100% sure, but from what he could see, Maya had snuck out of work to smoke a joint. His heart swelled with affection.

No, not affection, he told himself. Maybe…lust? Or no,

not lust. Something more friendly. Admiration? Respect? Something that made his chest feel all warm.

Maya took a long drag, held it in her lungs, then exhaled. Then she saw Tanner and froze. He smiled and gave her a small wave, and after a pause, she raised her arm and waggled her fingers in a wave back. She looked left and right, then raised her finger to her lips in a "sh" gesture. Tanner echoed it, and even across the street, he could see her hint of a smile.

Tanner climbed down from the ladder. He had to get his head on straight. He turned away from the window and pulled out his phone. Camille didn't answer again, so he sent her a text, and then, in anticipation of her next visit, he started looking at beds online. He quickly realized that he hadn't ever actually bought his own bed. He'd always just crashed on friend's couches or on whatever bed was free.

He scrolled through Facebook marketplace, looking at the bed frames and box springs people had listed. Almost all of them were in Silver Falls—he knew he'd probably have to take his truck down to pick things up for the old schoolhouse renovation there anyway, so he might as well make a trip of it. He was about to put his phone away when an ad caught his eye.

It was an old four-poster bed, deep reddish wood, with leaves and branches carved into the posts. The headboard had an elaborate pattern of grapes and leaves, the stain darker in the deeper parts of the carving. It had just been listed that morning.

Tanner flipped through the pictures on the listing. It was at least $200 more than he wanted to pay, but something about the bed just captured him. He wanted it. It was stupid and expensive, and he wanted it anyway. And the listing was here in West Tindale. After his conversation with Billy about the "want list," Tanner sent the standard message of "Hey is this still available?" and waited.

His phone dinged within seconds.

"Yes, it's available! Can you pick it up tomorrow?"

Tanner knew the standard thing to do here was negotiate price, but he simply replied, "Done. I can do Venmo, cash, or check."

"Venmo works great. I'm here anytime between 9 and 3."

"Works for me," Tanner replied.

He put his phone away and smiled, then got back to hanging the curtains.

CHAPTER 11

A Tall Glass of Water

MAYA

A full week had passed since Maya's parents had given her a blank check, and she still hadn't spoken to Tanner about the old schoolhouse. She'd spent the entire time trying to come up with what to say…something that she hadn't already said. (And something better than "We'll do this the hard way.")

In the late afternoon, Maya finally sat down in her room with her altar. She laid out the three tarot cards from her last reading: The Chariot, the Knight of Swords, and The Tower. She realized that the night she met Tanner, she'd been in this same position…sitting cross-legged in her room, doing a spell before going to meet up with Anne at the bar. Except this time, she wasn't doing a spell to manifest getting laid.

Well, she hadn't gotten laid, but maybe Cora would be working again tonight. There was still time. She hadn't texted or called, but Maya was still hopeful. Right now, though, Maya was focusing on a different spell. One for clarity and guidance. She held lodolite and sodalite crystals in one hand, and laid her other hand over her heart. She took deep breaths and pictured Tanner standing in front of her. She tried to let the right words come to her…the words she could say to Tanner to get him to change his mind and sell her family the old schoolhouse.

But trying to think clearly while envisioning Tanner standing in front of her was proving…difficult. Her mind kept wandering to how striking his hazel eyes were, how much space he took up, the timber of his rich voice…

"Fine," Maya finally whispered to herself. "I give up. I'm going to the bar to meet with Anne," she said to the tarot cards in front of her. "And to maybe chat up Cora."

When she opened the door to the bar, though, there was no Cora in sight. There was Anne at a booth, and sitting at the bar nearby, was Tanner Sullivan.

"Goddammit," Maya whispered. She dipped her head to hide her face and slid into the booth with Anne.

"Hey," Anne said, then immediately lowered her voice and leaned over the table. "Have you seen that huge, delicious glass of water at the bar?! Curly hair, beard?"

Maya glanced over. There was only one man matching that description in this bar.

"Yes," Maya said.

"Since I'm not single, you need to go over there and chat him up for the both of us."

"That will not be happening," Maya said.

"Why not?"

"Because," Maya replied, "That is Tanner Sullivan."

Anne stared at her for a moment, her mouth open in disbelief. Anne looked from Maya to Tanner and back to Maya again.

"Jesus Christ," she said. "You didn't tell me he was so…that."

"Whose side are you on?!" Maya demanded.

Anne glanced back at Tanner, and Maya's eyes followed her gaze. His back was to them, and Maya could clearly see the width of his shoulders, muscles ready to shift and tighten beneath his shirt.

"I'm just saying," Anne whispered, her eyes still on Tanner. "Maybe you should seduce him after all."

"I am getting a drink," Maya said, standing and striding over to the bar. She walked all the way over to the far end of the bar, close to the jukebox and the bathrooms, as far away from Tanner as she could get. After placing her order, she risked a glance down the bar again. Tanner was still there. No book, no phone, just a…was that a can of Dr Pepper in front of him? Maya recognized the man sitting a few seats down from where she was standing, between her and Tanner.

"Hiya, Kenny," she said. He was reading a book, his glasses perched on his nose, a beer in one hand. He looked up.

"Hey, Maya," he said. "How're your folks?"

"Good," she said.

"Heard y'all were planning to buy the old school-house," Kenny said.

Maya blinked at him for a moment. She wasn't sure where he had gotten his information. Maya didn't think her parents had told anyone. They certainly hadn't told the real estate agent before the morning they tried to make the purchase. Maybe Ruby told Kenny? It took Maya a moment to figure out a diplomatic answer.

"Working on it," she finally said. She stepped away from the bar and turned to rejoin Anne at their booth.

But instead, she found herself face-to-face with Tanner. Apparently, when he'd stood up, it wasn't to leave, but to walk towards the bathrooms behind her.

"Did you just say something about the old schoolhouse?" he asked. Maya stared at him for a long, long moment. Then she grabbed Tanner's arm and dragged him into the hallway. Or, rather, she held his arm while he let himself be dragged. She wasn't sure she'd be able to move him if he didn't want to be moved.

The background noise of the bar was a little quieter as they stood in the dim hallway, looking at one another. Maya was sure she'd had some sort of speech ready to deliver, but now she just stood there, breathing a little heavier than she should be.

"Yes?" Tanner finally said, his eyebrows arched at her.

"You…" Maya began.

Tanner just stood there, waiting. It was maddening.

"You," she began again, this time pointing an accusatory finger. "You are…infuriating."

This isn't what Maya had planned to say, but it was what came out. Tanner stared at her for a moment, then frowned.

"I'm infuriating?" he said. "Why am I infuriating?"

"Because," Maya said, lowering her finger. "Because you're here, in this bar, and you're all tall and everything, and it's completely…it's just…uncalled for."

None of this was going well. At all. Maya prided herself on being able to come up with zingers on the spot, but apparently now was not one of those times. Try as she might to come up with some brilliant and biting remark, her brain refused to work.

Maya was sure she saw a hint of a smile play around Tanner's lips. "I'm infuriating because I'm…tall?"

"You know what I mean."

Tanner quirked an eyebrow at her. "No, I don't know what you mean."

Maya stood, arms crossed, chest heaving, and stared at

Tanner for a full ten seconds. When he took one small step towards her, her breath caught.

"What do you want, Maya?" Tanner asked, his voice low. Maya could feel the rumble of it in her chest, in the place between her legs.

Okay. Well. What she wanted, she could admit in this moment, was to climb him like a tree. To grab the front of his shirt and pull him into one of the bathrooms and kiss him until neither of them could think straight. She wanted him to lift her off her feet and fuck her against the wall while she screamed his name.

But Maya didn't say any of this. Instead, she turned on her heel and strode back out into the bar, and threw herself down into the booth across from Anne. She rested her elbows on the table and put her head in her hands.

"Everything okay?" Anne asked slowly. Maya raised her head to look at her best friend.

"Fine! I admit it!" Maya exploded in an exaggerated whisper. "He's a delicious glass of water and it's hard to talk to him when he's being a delicious glass of water!"

Anne stared blankly. "That's…not what I asked, but I definitely understand."

Maya glowered at the table.

"So how are we feeling about Operation Carte Blanche?" Anne asked, with a hint of a smile.

"What's Operation Carte Blanche?" a voice near them said. Maya looked up to see Anne's mom, Debbie, sliding into the booth next to Anne. "But more importantly," she added, lowering her voice, "Have we talked about the absolute four-course meal of a man at the bar?"

"Mom!" Anne laughed, while Maya threw up her hands.

"Not for me, for one of you girls!"

"I am married to Roberto," Anne said.

"For Maya, then," Debbie said. And suddenly she was standing up and walking purposefully towards the bar. By the time Maya realized what was happening, it was too late to stop her.

Within thirty seconds, Debbie was steering Tanner Sullivan toward their booth. Debbie slid in next to Anne again, and Tanner paused before taking the seat next to Maya.

"Tanner, this is my daughter, Anne," Debbie said.

"Nice to meet you, Tanner," Anne said, and Maya tried to shoot her a look.

"Nice to meet you, Anne," Tanner said. He reached over to shake Anne's hand, and his leg brushed against Maya's for a split second. She could feel the heat of him next to her, and it made her feel like someone had taken a soda bottle and shaken it up inside her chest.

"And Maya is my other daughter," Debbie added. "Not by blood, but by spirit—she's a girl after my own hippie heart."

Maya loved Debbie with a fierceness beyond words, but just now, she wished that Debbie would be quiet.

Tanner glanced down at Maya—he had to, because he was a whole head taller than her. "Nice to see you again," he said. He took a long pull from his Dr Pepper.

"Oh, do you know each other?" Debbie exclaimed.

"We've met," Tanner said. "A few times, actually." He was looking at Maya and Maya was having a hard time looking away.

"Has she given you a tarot reading yet?" Debbie asked. "I've been meaning to have you do another one for me," she added, turning to Maya. "She's got a real gift."

Anne was suppressing a smile. "Hey Mom, can I stop by the bookstore? I want to grab something from upstairs."

"Right now?" Debbie asked.

"Mm hm," Anne said.

"Are you sure you need to leave *right now*?" Maya said.

Debbie glanced at her daughter, then at Maya and Tanner, and her eyes went wide. She stood up and dragged Anne up with her. "Oh! Yes, we do need to leave right now! Bye, Maya! Love you!"

"Will you be back?" Maya asked Anne, a hint of pleading in her voice.

"Probably not." When Maya didn't say anything, Anne added, "Consider it payback for Silver Falls." She winked as she walked away.

Maya wanted to point out that intentionally throwing Anne and Roberto together in Silver Falls two years ago was a completely different situation, but she didn't want to bring it up in front of Tanner. She glanced over at him, and he didn't move, even though the two of them were now crowded into one seat.

"What happened in Silver Falls?" he finally asked.

"Nothing," Maya grumbled.

"Okay," Tanner replied. They sat in silence for a few more moments, Tanner slowly sipping his drink. Finally, he glanced over and then rose. Maya breathed a sigh of relief, but in another moment, he was sitting across from her.

"Are you seriously drinking a Dr Pepper?" she asked. "What are you, a teenager?"

Tanner glanced down at the can, then back up at her. "Is drinking a Dr. Pepper against the rules or something?"

Maya rolled her eyes. "Why go to a bar if you're not going to drink?"

Tanner shrugged, then smiled at her. "I guess I just like the company."

And then he winked.

And Maya felt it in every cell of her body.

A buzzing sound came from Tanner's pocket. He

pulled his phone out and then glanced up. "Sorry, I have to take this. My girlfriend."

And then he stood up, leaving Maya to feel a whole lot more than she thought she would about the word "girlfriend."

CHAPTER 12

The Phone Call

TANNER

"Hey, sweetheart," Tanner said.

"Hi," Camille replied. Tanner squinted into the sunlight outside the bar, his chest flooding with warmth. He hadn't realized how much he'd missed hearing Camille's voice. He thought of her warm red hair and the way her eyes went soft when she smiled.

"I've missed you," he said.

Tanner became aware of silence on the other end of the line, and pulled his phone away from his ear to glance at it for a moment.

"Hon? Are you still there?"

"I'm still here," Camille said. "That's um…that's what I'm calling to talk to you about."

Tanner's stomach sank inexplicably, but he tried to ignore it.

"That you're still there?" he said.

Camille was quiet for a moment before replying, "Yes." Another long pause. "I don't know how to…I'm…I think I need to stay here."

Tanner tried to understand what Camille was talking

about. "Are you saying you won't be able to make it out to visit?"

Camille didn't answer.

"Camille?"

"This isn't working, Tanner."

This time Tanner was the one who was quiet. "The distance?" he asked.

"Any of it," she replied.

Tanner paused for a long time. "I don't...I don't know what to say," he finally said. "I know I'm not always the best boyfriend, but—"

"You're not my boyfriend," Camille replied.

Her words cut through Tanner so violently that for a moment, he couldn't breathe. It was true that she never used the word "boyfriend" when talking about him, but she'd never outright *denied* it. Tanner tried to steady his voice when he spoke next.

"I've called you my girlfriend for over a year. If you didn't want to be my girlfriend, why didn't you say anything?"

"You...You're someone I was dating," Camille's voice shook a little. Tanner couldn't find words to respond, so Camille spoke again. "This is what I mean. You deserve someone who...you deserve to be someone's boyfriend. I just don't think...I want you to be mine."

Tanner held the phone to his ear for a few more moments. Neither of them spoke for a long time. Finally, Camille broke the silence.

"I don't have any of your stuff over at my place, and I don't think you have any of mine. So I think this can just be it. Let's just make it a clean break."

Tanner nodded before he remembered that Camille couldn't see him, then said, "Okay."

"Would it be okay if we didn't talk for a few months?"

"Okay."

Camille paused. "Goodbye, Tanner."

It took Tanner a moment to reply, but by the time he managed to say, "Bye, Camille," she had already hung up.

Tanner stood outside with his phone in his hand for a long time. He felt rooted to the spot. But after the initial shock of what had just happened wore off, Tanner was surprised to find that he didn't feel...that bad? Which he then felt bad about. The thing that had hurt the most was Camille not being willing to say that he was her boyfriend. The revelation that he might not be "boyfriend material" in her eyes. The fact that it was *Camille* saying it didn't seem to matter. As he tried to think about his life over the next little while (and probably forever) without Camille, it felt...okay.

But still. Being dumped over the phone by the person you'd been dating for over a year didn't feel completely great. His ego felt a little bruised. He would probably need a day or two to get his feet under him again. He started walking towards home.

It was times like this he wished he could call Billy without racking up ridiculous phone charges. He kept replaying his and Camille's conversation in his head, brief as it was. Yes, it sucked that he had just been dumped. And it super definitely sucked that after all this time, she still wouldn't claim him as hers. But he also felt an unexpected...lightness.

Maybe he hadn't loved Camille as deeply as he thought he did. The idea flooded him with guilt. But if he was willing to be fiercely honest with himself, he and Camille weren't exactly a great match. If you had asked Tanner to describe his ideal girlfriend, he couldn't say for sure that he'd describe Camille. Of course he had loved her. But maybe not quite enough. And he wanted someone to love him enough to be called his.

And if that was the case…in a way, her breaking up with him was a kind of gift. Camille had always been caring, and she had been caring to the end—he did deserve to be someone's boyfriend, even if it wasn't Camille's. Maybe he could find someone who would be willing to be his girlfriend in the way that he wanted to be a boyfriend.

Tanner stopped in his tracks.

Maya.

He felt his whole soul pause. One held breath before…

If Tanner let this breath out, with Maya's name on it, he could tell that there was a chance of floodgates opening. Of more longing than he'd dared to acknowledge rushing to the surface. He had already fully admitted to himself that he was attracted to her, and had carried guilt about it for the past few weeks. But now that he was actually free to feel it without guilt, he was worried that it might turn into more than just attraction.

Maya was so…fierce. Everything about her was so alive. She was so quick to say what she was thinking. And she was beautiful, but there was a power to her beauty. Like a goddess who could become vengeful if wronged.

Tanner started walking again.

What would things with Maya even look like? How would that even start? How *could* that even start? He didn't think Maya outright hated him, but they weren't exactly friends. He couldn't quite figure out next steps. Could he ask for her number…? Why would he ask for her number? Should he go back to the bar and tell her that he didn't have a girlfriend after all?

Times like this Tanner wished he drank.

But he knew what Len was like with a bottle in his

hand, and he also knew that he had the same thing in his own blood, right under the surface.

Tanner got within one block of his apartment and stopped.

What was he going to do when he got home? Sit around feeling guilty that he didn't feel worse about Camille breaking up with him? Sit around feeling like shit because maybe he wasn't boyfriend material? Ruminate about Maya?

Nah, he had to work this out in his usual way. He turned around and started walking back to the old schoolhouse.

As he measured and cut and sketched, he thought about Camille. How they'd met, the year that they'd spent together. What it was about her that had drawn him in. There was a softness to her that he'd wanted to protect. And she had such a caring soul. After the chaos of his childhood and teenage years, it was comforting to have someone there to just take care of him. But Camille was also…safe. She never disagreed with him on anything. Which was actually weird for a lawyer, if he really thought about it. If he really thought about it, he wasn't sure he even knew Camille that well. He didn't know what her favorite meal was or her favorite movie, what drove her crazy, what she was most afraid of.

And he was startled to realize that he hadn't thought to ask.

Guilt filled Tanner's stomach. Poor Camille. No wonder she hadn't thought of him as her boyfriend. He hadn't taken the time to really figure her out, or even get to know her.

Tanner sat down on a stool to think. He could definitely blame a significant portion of that neglect on himself. On the ways that he was raised to be a man, the things he was raised to think of as important. But if he really thought about it, a small part of him knew that deep down, part of the reason he hadn't tried to learn about Camille is that he just didn't quite care enough about her to find out.

Of course he cared about her. He did love her, in a generally affectionate sort of way. But there wasn't anything in their relationship that had driven him to find out more.

Tanner stood up and began pacing.

Okay, so he and Maya weren't exactly best friends, but he still wanted to get to know her. (And yes, fine, okay, he also wanted to fuck her brains out.) But he trusted he could be mature enough to think with his actual head, and not his dick, long enough to pursue a meaningful connection.

So he wasn't going to ask her out or anything right away. Or even at all, maybe. What if he just…asked questions? Let her talk. And if the opportunity for something more presented itself, he'd cross that bridge when he got to it. But for now, he'd just…try to get to know her.

She said something about his sign when they met in the Schoolhouse that one time. So he knew she was interested in astrology. Maybe he could start there. He pulled his phone out, searched for "astrology signs," and settled in to learn.

CHAPTER 13

The Thunderstorm

MAYA

Maya kept thinking about Tanner, about his girlfriend, about the way he'd winked at her in the bar. That had been three days ago, and it was still getting to her.

Maya loved that West Tindale National Park was literally right outside her back door. When she got back from college a few years ago, she'd begun this habit of wandering in the woods behind her family's hotel. There was no "official" trail, so technically it wasn't really allowed. But between the deer and the locals, a few faint footpaths had been carved out. Maya never went too far in, and she'd never been lost yet. And there was no place quite as good for thinking clearly without distractions. She left her phone in her room and walked downstairs, then headed into the shade of the trees.

Her feet scuffed against pine needles as she walked and thought about what to do next. She was no lawyer, but she couldn't imagine there was anything her family could do legally to get the old schoolhouse from Tanner. Maybe she just hadn't pleaded her case to Tanner well enough. She thought back to her first conversation with him. She had told him about zoning laws and location, but maybe she hadn't made it clear how important it was. How high the stakes were. She vaguely remembered saying the word "important" at some point but that was kind of all. (Aside from her stupid vague threat to "do things the hard way," which she still felt embarrassed about.)

The trees were tall and blocked out a decent amount of sun, but after a few minutes of walking, Maya looked up to realize that the sky was darkening. She heard a low rumble of thunder in the distance. She smiled to herself. Thunderstorms in West Tindale Park didn't usually happen until July or August, so getting one in early May was a treat. Maya loved thunderstorms.

Another roll of thunder passed overhead, this one a little louder. Maya glanced over her shoulder toward town, and when she felt the first drop of rain, she decided to head back. And it was a good thing, too, because in a matter of minutes, it was pouring, and Maya was soaked through. She held her forearm over her eyes to try and shield them from the rain, but it was already almost impossible to see.

"Goddammit," she said, trying to keep her eye on the path below her feet. The ground was soon becoming too muddy to walk easily, and the path was quickly disappearing. There was really no way to tell which direction she was going. She stopped and tried to look up to see if there were any large trees nearby where she could take shelter until the worst of the storm had passed, but she kept having to swipe her hair out of her eyes. She couldn't remember if she'd ever seen it rain this hard.

Maya stood and thought. The storm couldn't last forever, and she probably wouldn't actually die if she had to stay in it for a little while. And she could try to follow the path, but the chances of her losing it and wandering into the park were higher than normal. She was standing and trying to decide what to do, when she was startled by a hand on her shoulder.

Maya jumped and screamed, and was about to start swinging when she recognized the tall figure in front of her.

"Tanner?" she said. She practically had to yell to be heard over the storm.

"Come on!" he said. "There's a tree over here!"

He held out his hand. Maya hesitated, and then she took it. Tanner led them a few yards off the path to a large pine, its branches thick and spread wide, creating a small circle of protection close to its trunk. Maya bent over, squeezing the water out of her hair. When she stood back up, Tanner was standing a few feet away and looking at her with an expression she couldn't quite read. His brown curls were wet, and water dripped down his face. Maya's eyes roamed over the drops near his temples, at the hollow of his throat.

"What are you doing out here?" she finally asked. Here in the shelter of the pine, the rain was muted slightly.

"I could ask you the same question," Tanner said.

"I was going on a walk."

"So was I."

The two of them looked at one another for a moment. Then Maya glanced out at the rain, still coming down in sheets. She sank down to the dry(ish) ground and sat with her back leaned against the trunk of the tree. After a moment, Tanner joined her. She was suddenly aware of the heat of his body, close next to her.

"Thanks," Maya said. "By the way. I guess."

"No problem," Tanner said.

Maya glanced at him. He was running a hand through

his hair, shaking the water out of it. His hazel eyes were gazing out at the rain.

"I'm not a damsel in distress," she said.

Tanner looked over at her. Maya had to stop her breath from catching. She hadn't realized how close they were sitting.

"I didn't need rescuing," she managed to continue. "But I'm glad you…but I…thank you."

Tanner nodded, then turned his face back towards the park. He leaned his head back against the trunk of the tree. "I know you're not a damsel in distress, but I do keep rescuing you, don't I?"

Maya frowned. "When else have you rescued me?"

Tanner turned to her, searching her face for a moment. "That night at the bar. When that drunk guy wouldn't leave you alone."

Maya was stunned. Her frown deepened, and she felt anger flood her chest. "Oh, was that what you did?" she said. "You stick up for some fellow asshole misogynist who wouldn't leave me alone, then glare at me like I wouldn't give this poor guy a chance? You call that 'rescuing me'?"

Tanner's face mirrored Maya's frown. "I was…" he started. Maya watched him turn away and swallow hard.

"I didn't mean to glare at you," he said.

Maya felt her irritation deepen. "Then what do you call what you did?"

Tanner drew his knees up a little and rested his forearms on them. She watched as he traced a long scar on the side of one hand. "Engaging the aggressor," he said quietly.

"What?"

"I don't know what it's actually called, but I just…I know that sometimes when women reject men, they can get…violent. Or dangerous. The men can, I mean. And they do the same thing when someone confronts them about what they're doing. So if you can sort of…distract the aggressor, it's easier to keep everything calm. I didn't want anyone to get hurt, so I just started talking to the guy to give you a chance to get out of there. If you needed it."

For a long time, Maya couldn't think of anything to say. Finally, she asked, "Why did you glare at me afterwards?"

Tanner shook his head. "I didn't mean to. I was trying to check in with you, make sure you were okay. Maybe my face just looks more glare-y than I realized."

Maya leaned her head back against the tree. She thought back to that night at the bar. Tanner's method had worked. She had been able to escape the drunk creep who wouldn't leave her alone, and no one had gotten violent or threatening.

"Why didn't you just punch the guy?" Maya asked.

Tanner looked at her and she saw something pass over his face. "I wanted to," he said quietly. "I just thought the other method would work better in the long run."

"You should tell people that that's what you're doing," she said.

He smiled at her, and the sight of it filled Maya's blood with what felt like champagne fizz. His teeth were white and straight, but it was the way his eyes crinkled, the way his whole face changed when he smiled. It caught Maya off-guard, and she couldn't quite think for a moment.

"It doesn't work as well if you tell people what you're doing," he said.

They stayed like that for a moment, sitting side by side, looking at each other, Tanner's smile warm and open, Maya's heart speeding up.

A clap of thunder startled them both out of their shared look.

"Good lord," Maya said, peering out at the storm. The

rain wasn't coming down any harder, but the thunder definitely sounded closer.

"I really hope the roof of the old schoolhouse doesn't leak," Tanner said. Then he glanced over at Maya. "Sorry," he said. "That was…sorry."

Maya felt everything in her deflate. "I hope the roof does leak," she said. She meant to sound snarky, but it came out more petulant than anything.

Tanner glanced over at her. "I'm sorry. About the old schoolhouse. It's just…it's important to me."

Maya got up and then sat directly across from Tanner.

"Why?" she said.

"Why what?"

"Why is it important to you? Tell me."

CHAPTER 14

Under the Tree

TANNER

T anner was taken aback. Both because he wasn't sure how to explain why the old schoolhouse was important to him, and also because of the way Maya had turned towards him. The amount of shelter the pine tree provided wasn't enormous, so in order to both stay out of the rain and face him, Maya had to practically sit between his ankles. His feet rested on either side of her wide hips as she sat cross-legged in front of him, her knees hovering over his ankles. Rain water still soaked her hair and clung in waves around her face, and she was gazing at him with a directness he wasn't used to experiencing from anyone. Tanner felt a growing tightness in his jeans, which he was trying very hard to ignore.

"I'm not sure where to start…" he said, shifting his legs so they were only on one side of Maya's hips. (Her perfect, wide hips…) If he was dealing with a situation in his jeans, he didn't want Maya to have a front-and-center view of it. It would also be easier to deal with said jeans situation if she wasn't sitting literally between his legs. He stretched one leg out in front of him, and brought the leg closest to Maya up so that he could rest his arm on his knee again.

"Start at the beginning," Maya said. "How long have you wanted to buy the old schoolhouse?"

Tanner looked up, a few small drops of water beginning to fall into their shelter. "I've only had the ability to buy it for a few months, but I've loved the building since I was fifteen. At least. Probably longer. Since I was really little."

"Why?"

Tanner paused and looked at Maya.

She folded her arms. "If you're going to take the old schoolhouse away from my family," she said, "I want it to be for a good reason. So is it a good reason?"

Tanner was quiet. He ran his thumb along the scar on his hand, not sure how much to share. Should he tell her about Len's death and the life insurance policy? About his brother in prison in California, who would need a place to work when he got out in a few years? About that afternoon when he was a teenager, standing in the empty building with his mom and brother, the rain pouring then just like it was now, when this daydream was first spoken aloud? About a whispered promise at his mom's casket?

"I have good memories of it," he said slowly. "When I was young, Len…my dad…I didn't always get along with my dad. But we would come to West Tindale every year, and there was one year when he couldn't come. So it was just me and my mom and my brother. We stopped by the building. My mom…my mom said something about wanting to turn the old schoolhouse into a coffee place. And now I have the means to do it."

"What does your mom think about that now?"

Tanner was quiet for another moment. "My mom passed away a few years ago. My dad died this past spring.

It's his life insurance policy that allowed me to buy the property."

Maya studied Tanner's face for a moment, then turned her head and looked out at the rain. Tanner's eyes roamed over her profile. She was this stunning combination of hard angles and softness. Sharp jawline. Full, wide lips. Strong nose, and large, expressive eyes. For some people, her features might be too…strong. But he found her face arresting. Right now, her expression was hard to read. She looked back at him. Tanner swallowed, but held her gaze.

"Where are you from?" she asked.

"California," Tanner replied. "Where are you from?"

"Here," Maya said. "Although I went to college in Boston. Hotel Management. Very exciting." She rolled her eyes. "It wasn't the best, but now I can help my parents run the hotel."

Tanner liked this. He liked Maya. Even though he wasn't sure if she still hated him. He actually wasn't sure if she hated him to begin with, but at least they were friendlier now than when they first met. Maybe they could become real friends. And, he reminded himself, if she wasn't into men, then it was safe and perfectly innocent.

"What would you do?" he asked. "If you didn't have to work for your parents' hotel?"

"I'd run a shop in town," Maya said. She said it quickly, with no hesitation. Then her hand flew to her mouth. She looked stricken, as if she'd been caught saying something she shouldn't. Like if you had said something rude about someone and then discovered that they were standing right behind you. It took her a minute to regain her composure.

"What kind of shop?" Tanner asked.

Maya paused before replying. "I make soaps," she said. "And lotions. Candles. Lip balms. I sell them at the hotel and at a few different places in town. But I'd love my own shop."

"Why don't you do it?" Tanner asked.

Maya looked at the ground. "You don't know my parents," she said. "They worked so hard for us kids, for my brother and me to have this better life. They grew up so poor. And the hotel needs me. We're struggling enough as it is. And I didn't want to disappoint my parents. I can't disappoint them." She looked up at him and gave him a small, sad smile. "And it's all right. Really. I think they're beginning to let go of me and Devan a little bit. Now that we're actually adults, even though sometimes they don't seem to remember that."

Now that Tanner had learned a little bit about Maya, he wanted to know more. "Tell me about your parents."

Maya shrugged. "Not much to tell," she said. "Harriet and Bruce Clark grew up in West Tindale, met in high school, got married, and bought the hotel. They had me and Devan, and now all four of us run the hotel together when we're not driving each other crazy." Maya shifted, leaning back on her hands. It made the still damp fabric of her shirt cling to her body, and Tanner could faintly see the outline of her bra. He quickly looked at the ground. "What's your brother like?" she finally said.

Tanner looked up at her. He took another deep breath. "He's in prison in California," he said. "He's a good guy, deep down. Maybe even not deep down, maybe just… actually a good guy. He just does dumb things. He got four years for aggravated assault, and he's got about three years left. We were always close growing up, even when he was being a dumbass, which was most of the time. He's still a dumbass most of the time," Tanner added, thinking of the contraband cell phone his brother had somehow gotten ahold of.

Maya nodded, then turned and looked out at the rain. Tanner followed her gaze, and the two of them sat in comfortable silence for a few moments. (Well, not completely "comfortable." Tanner was still aware of the proximity of her body to his, of the heat radiating from her, like there was a current of electricity flowing in the spaces where they were close to touching.)

"What about your brother?" Tanner asked.

Maya turned and smiled at him. "Devan is also a dumbass," she said. Tanner liked her smile. They held each other's gaze for a long moment.

Finally, Maya turned and looked out into the woods. "The rain's slowed down," she said.

Tanner looked outside of their small circle of shelter. Maya was right. There were still a few raindrops going down, but it was nothing compared to the downpour from earlier. He stood. "Clear enough to see our way home," he said, standing. He held his hand out to help Maya up. She looked at his hand, then at his face. She seemed to hesitate for a moment, then she reached out and placed her hand in his. He hauled her up, but she stumbled slightly when she got to her feet. She ended up pressed against him, their hands joined in between their bodies. Tanner looked down at Maya. He was at least a foot taller than her, so he really did have to look down. But her face was tilted up towards him, her large brown eyes moving over his face.

He was aware that the socially acceptable amount of time to be standing like this had passed, but he felt suspended in the moment. He swallowed again. A lock of Maya's hair had fallen into her face, and for a brief moment, he reached out as if to brush it aside, then quickly put his hand back down.

Maya blinked up at him. "I…"

This was not the afternoon that Tanner was expecting.

Nothing about Maya was expected. They were still standing pressed together, neither one of them moving. Tanner could feel the heat of her body along his front, awakening something in his chest.

Maybe she wasn't only into women. The way she was looking at him right now, her mouth slightly open, her breathing a little stronger than it had been a moment before, made him think she might also be into men. He could envision pressing her against the trunk of this tree, making quick work of her clothes, running his hands and his lips up and down her body until she was quivering beneath him.

Maya's body was still pressed against his. His eyes flicked down to her lips, and he saw her see it. Her mouth was slightly open and her lips looked so soft…

He felt her breath grow rapid as his gaze moved from her lips to her eyes. It would be so easy to close the distance between them, to taste the rainwater on her skin. Neither of them moved for a long moment, some invisible force suspended between them.

Then Maya pulled away and looked at him. Tanner could see a debate playing across her features. Finally, she bit her lip, and then turned and walked out into the woods.

CHAPTER 15

The Bar

MAYA

Good lord.

When Maya got home, she took the stairs two at a time. She slammed her bedroom door behind her and began peeling her wet clothes off, leaving them in heaps on the floor. She'd throw them in the dryer downstairs later.

Right now she was, apparently, too turned on to think straight.

Who did he think he was?! He was so…stupidly tall. And big. And standing pressed against him under that tree, for a long moment, Maya had wanted Tanner Sullivan to kiss her. Girlfriend or no girlfriend. Maya crawled into her bed and reached over to her nightstand to pull her vibrator out of the drawer.

She ran her hands over her skin, still damp from the storm.

What would it have been like? If Tanner had kissed her under that tree? He smelled like pine and some hint of spice she couldn't quite put her finger on. She imagined him pushing her back against the rough bark and devouring her mouth. He could probably tear her clothes right off her if he wanted to. If she wanted him to. Literally. She pictured him grasping her shirt and yanking it open, buttons flying, his large hands cupping her breasts.

Maya didn't often daydream about being outright ravished, but something about Tanner awoke a desperation in her. She wanted him towering over her, crouching to get to her, devouring her whole. Standing there under that tree with him, pulled flush against his height, she'd had visions of reaching out to unbuckle his belt. Of begging him to unzip his pants and push his length into her, to feel his hardness in her most sensitive places.

Her hands moved the vibrator faster between her legs, her arousal building as she imagined herself and Tanner, their bodies slick with rain, moving together under the tree. Within seconds, Maya's climax came crashing over her, her legs shaking with release.

She lay panting, staring up at the ceiling, for a long while afterward. Finally, she sat up and set her vibrator on her nightstand. She closed her eyes. "Fuck you, Tanner Sullivan," she whispered.

LATER THAT AFTERNOON, she texted Anne.

> Update: Tanner has a girlfriend.

> How do we feel about that?

Maya thought for a moment.

> We feel neutral about that.

Which wasn't a lie, exactly. It's just that she had both

strong negative feelings and strong positive feelings and so she figured they cancelled each other out. She disliked that Tanner had a girlfriend, for reasons she didn't feel like exploring. And she was also relieved. If he had a girlfriend, she didn't *have* to explore any of her other feelings. They were already taken care of by his unavailability, *and* she didn't have to think about seducing him.

Anne saw right through her.

> We are disappointed in not seducing him aren't we

Maya sighed.

> Fine. Correct. Yes. Shut up.

Maya didn't see Tanner for a full five days. She went to work, she went to her room. She was occasionally aware of the sounds of construction coming from the old schoolhouse, which she chose to actively ignore.

But West Tindale was one square mile, so it was only a matter of time until Maya was sitting across from Anne at a booth at the bar, and Tanner walked in.

He was even taller than she'd remembered.

Maya felt a slight pinch in her nipples, an urge to clench her thighs together. She wanted to run her hands through his curly hair so desperately that she had to sit on her hands.

Anne clocked Tanner right away. "If it isn't Mr. Schoolhouse," she said quietly. "With…Cosimo?"

Maya's gaze snapped up. What the hell was Tanner doing with Cosimo? The two of them were chatting easily, making their way to the bar. Maya resisted scowling. She and Cosimo had grown up together. He was her best friend's brother-in-law. He was family. Was this man going to just waltz into town and take *everything* that was hers?

She refused to look at him.

"It's really a shame about Tanner's girlfriend," Anne added in a whisper. "He would be fun to seduce."

"Stop it."

"Maya, it has been weeks since your parents gave you a literal blank check and instructions to get the old schoolhouse back from Tanner Sullivan and I have seen you make zero progress on that goal."

Maya glared at her friend. "I have made attempts! I just didn't tell you about them. Besides, I don't see you suggesting anything other than seducing him, which we know is off the table."

"Just go talk to him."

"I don't want to."

"Yes, you do."

Maya glared again, and Anne just rolled her eyes. "I'll get rid of Cosimo. Go get your drink order from the bar and talk to the man about the goddamn old schoolhouse."

And then Anne stood up, and much to Maya's annoyance, walked over to the two men sitting at the bar. Maya watched Anne smile and hug her brother-in-law, then say something to Tanner. Maya was in the middle of trying to formulate a plan to get Anne to stop whatever she was doing, when Cosimo and Anne walked out of the bar.

Maya grimaced at the table and thought about following Anne out. But something in her was making a different decision, and she found herself standing and walking to the bar. The stool next to Tanner was open, so Maya sat in it.

"Hey," he said.

Maya turned and leaned her head on one hand, facing him. "Hi," she said.

Tanner's eyes moved over her features, as if he was cataloguing them. Maya shifted slightly in her seat. The moment was broken when the bartender set Maya's drink down in front of her.

"You had the rum and coke, right?" he said. Maya looked up. She didn't recognize the bartender…he must be another one of the twentysomethings who came up for the summer.

"Yeah," she said.

Tanner raised his Dr Pepper to her. She took her glass and clinked it against the can.

"Cheers," he said, before taking a swig. Maya watched his throat as he swallowed, the muscles and tendons in his neck straining slightly. She had the insane impulse to lean forward and lick the little divot below his Adam's apple. When he lowered his drink, he looked at her.

"Were you going to drink that?" he asked.

Maya startled and then took a sip. A too large, too fast sip. She covered a cough with her arm.

"All right?" Tanner asked, amusement in his voice.

"Fine," Maya said, gulping down half her rum and coke to prove it.

"Good," Tanner said, taking another leisurely sip.

Maya was aware of how close their legs were. If she moved her knee just a few inches to the left, it would bump up against his strong thigh. The thought sent heat rushing through her blood.

"So is there a reason you came over here, or…?"

There was that voice again. Maya wondered if a voice alone could make you come. She suddenly pictured Tanner standing behind her while she sat on the barstool, his hands running down her sides, his nose brushing her neck. She could picture him whispering into her ear, she could imagine feeling the vibration of his words against her back, his breath hot on her skin. He could reach down to slip his hand between her legs and she could lean back while he—

"Maya?" Tanner looked at her questioningly.

"What?"

"I asked if there was a reason you came over here."

"Why do you need to know?" she asked teasingly. "Need to make sure it's okay with your girlfriend?"

Tanner looked away. He took a swig from his Dr Pepper and studied the wall behind the bar.

"I don't have a girlfriend," he finally said.

Maya was unprepared for the effect this sentence would have on her. Her heart zoomed from the center of her chest to her toes, then up to the top of her head before crashing back down into her center.

"Didn't…didn't you say that was your girlfriend on the phone? The other day?"

Tanner still hadn't looked over at her. "We broke up," he said. "During that phone call actually."

Maya was trying to orient herself to this new reality in which Tanner didn't have a girlfriend. "Why?" She asked.

Tanner finally turned and fixed Maya in his gaze. She felt it in every muscle of her body, but didn't look away.

"She didn't want me as her boyfriend. I deserve to be with someone who wants me as a boyfriend," he said. He said it quietly, almost as if he was saying it to himself, except while looking at Maya.

Maya nodded. His answer hadn't given her nearly the level of detail she wanted, but she felt like she understood. She and Tanner sat at the bar and looked at each other for a moment. She laid her hand on his arm.

"I'm sorry," she said. And she was. Even though the knowledge that he was single was scrambling every single thing in her brain.

"Thanks," Tanner said.

Maya didn't move her hand away from his arm, and suddenly she was aware of the warmth of him under her touch. She thought that she should probably move her hand away, but she found that she didn't want to. She wanted to stay tethered to him somehow, letting whatever it was between them simmer for a few moments longer.

"Why didn't she want you to be her boyfriend?" Maya asked. The question came out before she had time to think too hard about it. Because she was having a hard time believing that someone could let a guy like Tanner go once she had him.

Tanner raised his eyebrows at her, then looked away. "I actually…I don't know. I didn't ask." He looked back at her, his hazel eyes roaming over her face. Every second she held his gaze felt like walking on a tightrope, and she didn't want it to stop. "I guess that was kind of the problem," he added.

"That you didn't ask?"

Tanner nodded, still looking at Maya. "I realized that I didn't really know her that well. And I didn't make the effort to find out. She was…safe. I wanted to take care of her, but without getting to know her."

It was Maya's turn to raise her eyebrows. "That is…"

"Shitty?"

"I was going to say that is very self-aware."

"Oh."

They looked at each other for a moment.

"How the fuck are you so self-aware?" Maya asked. "It's so…"

She was about to say "so hot" but she let her sentence trail off instead.

Tanner shrugged modestly. "I kind of didn't have a choice, the way I grew up," he said. "Or maybe I'd be like this anyway. I don't know. I just…can't help but notice how I'm feeling, I guess. Or how others are feeling."

Maya felt something warm swelling in her chest. This man. This tall, handsome, unexpected man. Sitting here in this bar with his can of Dr Pepper and his curly hair and his huge heart. His eyes searched hers for a moment.

"Hey," Tanner said.

"Hey," Maya replied.

"You didn't answer my original question," Tanner said.

Maya looked at him.

"Why you came over here."

Maya wasn't sure how to answer. She didn't actually know why she'd come over to sit next to Tanner. There were plenty of other seats at the bar if she wanted to stay. Instead, she was sitting here next to Tanner Sullivan, trying to simultaneously avoid and inhale his cologne, and thinking about how close their thighs were.

"I don't know why I came over here," Maya finally said, moving her hand away from his arm.

A brief smirk passed over Tanner's face, then he turned away and took another sip of his drink.

"Don't smirk at me!" Maya said.

Tanner turned back to her and fixed his hazel eyes on her. His next words were almost a whisper. "If you don't want me to smirk at you, is there something else you want me to do instead?"

CHAPTER 16

The Alleyway

TANNER

Tanner could not remember the last time he'd been this attracted to someone. He felt actually hungry for Maya, like his mouth needed to be filled with her as soon as possible. Her brown eyes were sparking with the same longing he felt in his chest and between his legs.

She stared at him now, and he didn't look away. Finally, Maya stood and grabbed his arm and started towards the door.

Tanner let himself be led. She dragged him out of the bar by his hand, and then turned the corner into a small alleyway. It was narrow, maybe five or six feet across, but enough dim light from a nearby streetlamp filtered through, allowing him to see her features.

It was chilly outside, the evening summer warmth still a month or two away. Maya let go of his hand, then stood looking at him for a moment. Finally, she backed up and leaned against one of the walls, her hands behind her back. Tanner stood, trying not to be obvious about the fact that he was watching her breasts rise and fall with her breathing. He was also having a hard time keeping his eyes

110

from dropping to take in the rest of her body…her hips, her legs.

When he spoke, it was quiet and honest. "What do you want?" When Maya didn't answer, he took one small step towards her. "I'm not asking that to be rude or anything. I actually want to know."

Maya looked at him for a long time, her eyes taking in all of him. Her answer was as quiet as his question had been. "Come here."

Tanner felt his blood rush. He thought vaguely of his plan to get to know Maya but he wasn't able to get his brain to hold that thought for very long. He took another step forward towards her. Her mouth fell open slightly, and he took another step, and another. Finally, he stood with his feet almost on either side of hers, crowding her against the alley wall. He placed his hands on the bricks above her. She didn't stop him.

Maya looked up at him and bit her lip, and Tanner stifled a moan. He loved how tall she made him feel, how protective. She slowly reached a hand out and placed it on his chest.

Tanner had never been this turned on by someone simply placing one hand on his chest, while they were both still fully clothed. When she reached another hand up and ran her palms up towards his shoulders, his eyes fell closed.

Her touch was like fire on his body, spreading heat to every corner of him. She was running her hands up and down, and he dropped his head back at the sensation. After a moment, he felt a slight tug near his collar and realized that Maya was pulling on his shirt to bring his face down closer to hers.

He opened his eyes to find her staring at his lips, and he smiled slightly. He reached one hand down to cup her face.

"Tell me what you want," he said. He drew his finger-tips down Maya's jaw, along her neck, over her collarbones. The shiver she let out at his touch was delicious. He wanted more.

"Tell me," he whispered, leaning forward to brush her ear with his lips.

Maya turned her head to the side to give him better access to her neck and made a small whimper of longing, and Tanner felt it in his jeans. He was already hard and getting harder. Did she have any idea how attractive she was?

"Please," he whispered. "Tell me what you want."

"I want…" Maya whispered, her voice slightly breathless.

"Yes?" Tanner asked, his nose trailing down the side of her neck. He wanted desperately to press his lips to the silky soft skin there.

"I want…" Maya said.

"Tell me."

"I want you…to…kiss me."

Maya barely got the words out before Tanner covered her mouth with his. He was hungry, almost desperate, and her soft warm lips molded against his just as eagerly. He had to crouch slightly to reach her. He pressed his tongue to the seam of her lips and she opened her mouth to him, their tongues tangling as he wrapped an arm around her waist. He had to brace himself against the wall with his other arm—he was afraid he'd fall over if he didn't.

Maya was running her hands through his hair, over his arms, taking in as much of him as she could. When he clutched her hips and shifted her body so that she was flush against him, against his growing hardness, she moaned into his mouth. His hands were aching to open her shirt, to slip into her jeans, to feel the heat of her on his fingers.

He felt her rock slightly against him before she pushed him away. Tanner stood staring at her from across the alleyway.

"We've got to stop," Maya said, her voice desperate. Her hair was disheveled, her lips red and so so kissable. She was staring at him from the other side of the alley, wild-eyed.

"Why?" Tanner asked, his own breath slightly ragged. He reached down to adjust himself, his cock pressed almost painfully against the fly of his jeans. He saw Maya's eyes flick downward, then back up to his face with a heated look.

"Because I…because I don't want to stop," she said.

Tanner grinned. He couldn't help it. He didn't want to stop either. He took a tentative step forward. "If you really want to stop, we can…" He ran a hand down her arm, then held her hand, running his thumb over her knuckles. He dropped his voice to a whisper and leaned forward. "But if you want me to ravish you in this alleyway, I am one second away from doing that."

Maya looked at him for what felt like an eternity. She didn't take her hand away.

"What do you want?" he said.

"I…I don't know," Maya said.

Tanner lifted her hand to his mouth and spoke quietly, brushing his lips along her palm. "I'll tell you what I want. I want to kiss you until you're dizzy. I want to press your body to mine until you forget everything but the feeling of me. I…" He paused, gauging Maya's response. She was staring at him with eyes full of lust, her mouth open as her breathing sped up. He said his next words in almost a whisper. "I want to make you come. I like to think I could make you come with just my tongue. Like this." And then Tanner sucked one of Maya's fingers into his mouth to show her, in exact detail, how he would make her come with his tongue.

Maya's eyes fell closed and she made a desperate kind of noise. Tanner had a sudden vision of Maya, her legs hooked over his shoulders, her back arching while he coaxed more of those noises out of her, until her silky soft thighs tightened around his head, her fingers clutching his hair.

The fact that she was in this alleyway with him now, her lips hot from his kisses, was incredible. The possibility that he could cover more of her with his lips was astonishing. He let her finger slip from his mouth and pressed a kiss to the wetness he had left there.

"Tell me what you want," he whispered.

Maya pulled her hand away and folded her arms. "Why do you keep asking me that?" she said.

Tanner stepped backward. "Because I want to know," he answered.

"I don't…" Maya cut herself off and looked at the ground. "I don't know how to answer. I don't even always know what I want." Tanner studied Maya as she slowly let the words form before speaking them. "It's so much easier to just do what someone else wants."

Tanner frowned at her. "But…the best thing is when someone tells you what they want, and you get to do it for them, and then you tell them what you want, and they do it for you."

"And if you don't want to do what they want you to?"

Tanner shrugged. "Then you say that."

Maya looked at the ground again. "You have no idea," she said, "how hard it is to say no. And how hard it is to say the things you want."

Something about those words filled Tanner with both heartbreak and rage. Maya struck him as so fiercely independent that it just made sense to him that she would just say and do whatever she wanted to. That's what she seemed to do in so many areas of her life. But he thought back to their conversation under the tree, about her downcast look when she talked about running her parents' hotel instead of owning her own shop. Maybe some wants were easier to say out loud than others. A thought occurred to him.

"Have you ever made a vision board?" Tanner asked, leaning against the opposite wall.

Maya pulled her coat closer around her as she looked up at him. It made him want to cross over to her and wrap her in his arms.

"A *vision board?*"

"My brother did this thing when he was at some juvenile detention group therapy thing. You cut out things from magazines and glue them to poster board and write down the things you want."

"I know what a vision board is."

Tanner smiled, remembering his conversation with Billy. "Well, you can also make a list. Like a…want list."

"Like a Christmas list?" Maya asked, smiling.

Tanner grinned. "Yeah. Like a Christmas list. Writing it down is like a way of practicing…wanting. Without worrying about how to make things happen. It's just stating what you want. There's almost…this is going to sound dumb, but there's almost a kind of magic in that. In saying what you want out loud. Or at least owning it."

It was quiet in the alleyway, as Tanner's words floated between them in the night air. Maya leaned her head back against the wall and sighed.

"A kind of magic," she repeated softly.

"Sorry," Tanner said. "I don't mean necessarily like, manifesting shit. Or, maybe I do. I don't know. I just mean there's something magic about saying what you want."

"No," Maya said, tilting her face forward to smile at him. "It's perfect. That makes perfect sense to me."

"Good."

The two of them looked at each other, and then Maya pushed away from the wall and crossed the few feet to Tanner's side of the alley. She stood in front of him for a brief moment, then turned and leaned against the wall beside him. She tilted her face up, and Tanner joined her, both of them gazing at the thin slice of sky above them, dotted with stars.

"What's on your want list?" Maya asked.

"I don't have one."

"But if you did."

Tanner didn't look at her as he answered, his eyes still on the sky above them. "To make sure my brother's okay. To make Sullivan's Coffee a place of safety and refuge." Tanner thought. "To get a couch for my apartment. To learn how to whittle."

Maya laughed softly. "What is it with men coming to West Tindale and wanting to whittle?"

"It's all the knife shops," Tanner said. Maya laughed again. "So?" Tanner said. "What's on your want list?"

Maya turned smiled at him, then stepped away from the wall until she was standing in front of him. "For you kiss me again."

CHAPTER 17

Checking In

MAYA

When Maya got to the top of the stairs hours later, she heard her name. She closed her eyes. "Shit," she whispered. It was late, and she was sure she looked mussed and over-kissed, but she couldn't pretend she hadn't heard her dad's voice. She ran her fingers through her hair, walked down to her parents' open bedroom door, then leaned on the doorframe. "Hey," she said.

Harriett and Bruce were both sitting up in bed, her with a laptop, him with a novel.

"Come in," Harriett said. "We wanted to check in with you."

Maya's stomach dropped, but she strode in and sat on the edge of the bed. "About what?"

Harriett set the laptop aside and leaned forward. "We were wondering if you had any luck with the old schoolhouse. With that Tony Sullivan fellow."

"Tanner Sullivan," Maya corrected.

"Yes, Tanner. Have you tried speaking with him lately?"

Maya wasn't sure how to answer this question. She had

definitely spoken with him, but not quite…about the old schoolhouse.

She shook her head and decided on a half-truth, minus a few key details. "I ran into him at the bar earlier tonight, but he left before I could talk to him about it."

Harriett sighed. "Well, I just think it's cruel of him," she said. "He has no consideration whatsoever for other people."

"He didn't know you were planning on buying the building," Maya pointed out.

"But afterward," Harriet said.

"Maybe he has his own reasons for wanting the old schoolhouse," Maya replied. She thought back to her conversation with Tanner under the tree, his story about his late mother loving the building, about the memories he had of this place.

"Well," said Harriett, "They can't be as good as our reasons."

Maya sighed.

"Just talk to him, honey," Bruce said, looking at her over his book.

"I will," Maya said. She stood up. "Good night."

When Maya got to her room and saw her reflection, she almost laughed out loud. Her lipstick was completely gone, her hair was a mess, and she was pretty sure that she had a hickey near her collarbone.

She hadn't expected his beard to be so soft. His arms to be so strong.

They'd made out in the alleyway for what could have been five minutes or possibly five hours. They'd only stopped when Tanner had put his hands on her shoulders, held her away from him and said, "You're driving me crazy. We've got to either stop or go someplace." Maya had grinned at him and then said they should probably stop. Even though she wanted his hands on her again.

Maya's head fell back in pleasure at the memory of him, and she reached into her nightstand drawer. Within only minutes, she was quivering on her vibrator.

As she lay in bed afterward, her breathing coming back down to normal, she thought about Tanner's "Want List." After spending a few hours with Tanner's hands roaming her body, she had a few things she could add to her own. She pulled out her journal and wrote "Want List" on the top of a new page.

I want Tanner Sullivan to make me come with his tongue.

I want Tanner Sullivan to fuck me.

I want

Maya wasn't sure what to write next. The main things on her mind were covered in the first two sentences she had written down. If she tried to extend her want list beyond Tanner Sullivan, she felt a slight recoil in her mind. If she tried to think about what she wanted for the future, she couldn't quite picture it. She couldn't quite remember the first time when she realized that her future had been decided for her, that the hotel was going to be her life. It had just always been true. Her parents had indulged her in other career aspirations when she was young, the way parents indulge a child who says they want to be a firefighter or a marine biologist when they grow up. When deep down, of course they didn't believe she was old enough to know what she wanted.

Maya didn't have a clear memory of being told an objective "no" when it came to anything else she wanted to do with her life. There was no moment of her parents sitting her down and explaining the facts of the family business to her. It was just that by the time Maya graduated high school, she knew that she was going to study hotel management and come back home and help run the Hitchin' Post Hotel.

Maya wasn't sure if a "Want List" could be retrospective. But Tanner said it could include impossible things. So Maya took a deep breath, and in small letters, she wrote "I want to run a soap shop in town." She closed her journal and fell asleep.

THE NEXT MORNING, after the heat and lust of the night before had sufficiently cooled (or at least cooled as much as could be managed), Maya took her parents' blank check in hand and walked over to the old schoolhouse. She had specifically waited until she saw Tanner's truck parked outside. She tried to concentrate on what she was planning on saying, and not just…eating Tanner whole. She straightened her shoulders and knocked on the old school-house door.

It took Tanner a few moments to answer, and when he did, Maya forgot how to think. His dark hair was full of dust, and stray curls were falling over his forehead and partly covering one of his hazel eyes. A thin sheen of sweat covered his face and bare forearms.

"Hi," he said, slightly out of breath. He grinned at her.

Maya blinked, mentally shaking herself. "Are you busy?" She asked.

Tanner glanced down at the sander in his hand, then back up at her, his grin widening. "I can take a break. What do you need?"

"I wanted to…would you be…" This wasn't going well. Maya's planned speech was nowhere to be found in any part of her brain, because Tanner was taking up the entire doorway and it was doing something to her breathing. She finally closed her eyes, literally blocking him out.

"I'd like to talk to you about the old schoolhouse again," she said. When she opened her eyes, Tanner was frowning.

"That's…not what I thought you were going to say," he said.

"I know. We can…first I wanted to talk to you about this."

"Is this the part where 'we do this the hard way'?" He said, a hint of teasing in his voice.

Maya felt her cheeks grow warm, partly out of embarrassment at her vague threat from earlier, and partly because Tanner had used the words "we," "do," and "hard," and she was apparently some sort of sex fiend who couldn't keep her mind out of the gutter. She took a breath.

"I'm not trying to…threaten you. Can I come in?"

Tanner stepped aside to let Maya through, then closed the door behind them. Maya stopped and took the room in. A lot had changed since the last time she was inside. The walls were now a deep blue, and the old fluorescent lighting fixtures had been torn out. Long yellow curtains hung at each of the tall windows, knotted up and away from the floor, which was covered with dust. A long wooden counter stood at the far end of the room, partly sanded.

"Wow," Maya said. She couldn't help it. It was becoming a truly beautiful space.

"Thanks," Tanner said.

The two stood in silence for a moment. The amount of work Tanner had already put into the building would make it even more difficult to convince him to sell it, but Maya told her parents she'd try. She pulled the check out of her pocket and showed it to him.

"We can pay up to $200,000," she said.

Tanner's eyes went from the check to Maya's face, his eyes slightly pained.

"I can't take your money," he said.

"It's not my money, it's my parents'. And it's not charity, it's to buy the building." Maya held the check out further, gesturing for Tanner to take it.

"Maya," he said.

Maya had been unprepared for the way her name sounded in his mouth. For the way his warm voice wrapped the two syllables up and presented them to her. She looked up into his face.

"Tanner," she said, quietly, like a test, like she was tasting his name out loud. She was still holding the check out. Something passed through his eyes, and he looked down at the check again. Tanner suddenly turned around and walked away from her, running his hands through his hair and growling in frustration. When he turned back to face Maya again, his eyes were almost pleading.

"I…can't," Tanner said. "I wish I could sell. I know it would mean a lot to your family and it makes sense. I wish I could make you happy. I just…"

Maya's brain snagged on "I wish I could make you happy" as Tanner trailed off. Did he mean her specifically? Or just the Clarks? Or maybe just…humanity in general? He seemed like the type to want to make humanity in general happy. That must be it.

"And," Tanner added, "It's only fair. I didn't know anyone else was interested in the building, and I got to it first."

Maya looked at him for a long moment, then sighed, and folded the check, putting in back into her pocket.

"Fucking Libras," Maya muttered.

"What?" Tanner said.

"I said FUCKING LIBRAS. Always about fairness," Maya folded her arms and looked at him.

Tanner gave her a small smile, and it knocked the wind out of her for a moment, which was really unfair, given the circumstances.

"What about my Capricorn moon or Scorpio rising?" he asked with a smirk, mirroring her position of folded arms.

Maya blinked. "What?"

"I looked it up," Tanner said, a little sheepishly. "After you asked me what time I was born. I looked up my chart." He bowed his head slightly, rubbing his neck and looking up at her through his curls. As much as he could for how tall he was.

Maya couldn't figure out which was more attractive: the way he was looking at her right now or the fact that he had looked up his birth chart because of their conversation. After a moment, she smiled back at him.

"Of *course* you're a Scorpio rising," she said.

They smiled at each other from across the room, a slow warmth building in Maya's chest.

"I mean, I don't really remember what any of it means," Tanner said. "But I remember those were my signs."

"Libras are all about balance," Maya said. "Justice and rationale and making sure everything is fair."

"What do the other signs mean?"

Maya could barely stand to be directly in the line of Tanner's attention like this. It had been a lot when he was kissing her in the alleyway, but this was different. It was too warm, too connected. But she didn't want to leave it, either. She thought back to looking up Tanner's sign all those nights ago.

"Your moon sign is your inner life…a deeper self. Capricorns are patient and hardworking and mature."

"And the Scorpio one?"

"Your rising sign is the vibe you give off. The face you present to the world."

"And what are Scorpios like?"

"Sexy," Maya said, before even thinking about it. Tanner raised his eyebrows at her, and she felt her cheeks warm for the second time that day. "And determined and mysterious," she added, but it didn't do much good. The word "sexy" hung in the air between them, an almost audible buzz.

Tanner's eyes roamed over Maya's face in the silence, and Maya could feel his gaze in her very bones. She was trying to keep her breathing normal, and she wasn't sure how well she was succeeding, because she felt a little dizzy.

"What's your sign?" He finally asked.

"I'm a Gemini," Maya said.

Tanner looked at her for a moment longer, then took one slow step towards her. "What are Geminis like?"

"Extroverted," Maya said. "Curious." Tanner took another step forward, his hands in his pockets. "Indecisive," Maya added.

"You don't seem indecisive to me," Tanner said quietly.

"It's the Aries moon," Maya said. She was a little afraid she was going to start rambling, because Tanner Sullivan was walking slowly towards her and she was supposed to be convincing him to sell the old schoolhouse and not thinking about his forearms or his eyes or the belt buckle that she suddenly desperately wanted to undo. "That's the bold, direct part of me."

Tanner stopped walking and stood a few feet away. "Well, you're certainly direct," he said, smiling.

CHAPTER 18

Poetry Night

TANNER

Tanner couldn't be certain, but he thought he saw Maya's face redden slightly. He wanted to offer her a drink or a chair or something—anything to get her to stay longer. Maya was still looking at him after he'd said that thing about her being direct.

"Thank you? I think?" Maya said.

"It was meant to be a compliment."

Maya scowled sarcastically at him. But he somehow still found himself liking the way her lips looked, the fire in her eyes, the way the light was hitting her brown waves of hair. He tried to stop his eyes from wandering down her figure, to the fullness of her hips, the curve of her thighs.

"Do you want to go for a walk or something?" Tanner asked.

Surprise flitted over Maya's face, and then she frowned. "Why?"

Tanner shrugged. "Get to know each other better," he said.

Maya studied his face. "I know you plenty," she said.

"You do?"

"Sure. We just talked about it. You're a Libra sun, Capricorn moon, Scorpio rising. You care deeply about your little brother, even though he's an asshole sometimes, just like mine is. You work hard. You care about fairness. You want everyone to feel safe and comfortable. And you're holding on to this damn building for all of those reasons, even though I've offered you two hundred thousand dollars in cash for it."

Tanner didn't know what to say. An unfamiliar warmth was spreading through his chest. Regardless of whether or not he believed in astrology, Maya's read felt startlingly accurate. He wasn't aware that Maya saw all that in him. Something about her speaking it out loud made him feel… he didn't even know. He rubbed his palm over the spot on his sternum that was feeling heavy with something.

"That's…" he started.

Maya folded her arms, looking satisfied. "I bet you don't know me," she said. "Besides the fact that I'm a good kisser," she added.

Tanner grinned, then put his hands in his pockets and looked at her. "I know you're fiercely loyal," he said. "You're determined and independent, even though your family makes it hard for you sometimes. You're funny and…quick-witted. You sacrifice a lot that people don't see, but it's all for the people who are important to you."

Maya stared at him. Tanner met her gaze, feeling suddenly like he'd just shed his clothing. Even though she was the one he was describing, the detail of his assessment revealed almost as much about him as it did about her. He hadn't realized what he knew went so deep, but he found himself speaking the words he'd been carrying for a while. He took his hands out of his pockets and stood awkwardly, shuffling from one foot to another, trying to figure out what to say next.

Suddenly Maya was striding towards him. He almost took a step backwards, but then suddenly, her arms had wrapped around him and she was burying her cheek against his chest. He was so surprised that he stood frozen in place for a moment, before lifting his arms to wrap them around Maya. They stood that way for one, two, three seconds, embracing. Tanner was filled with more of that strange warmth in his chest, but this time it was a sort of melting…a kind of coming home, or slipping into a hot bath, or being wrapped in a thick blanket. This was more than the heat of making out in an alley by a bar. He slowly began to move one hand up Maya's spine, but as soon as he'd moved an inch, she kept her arms around him but pulled away enough to look up at him.

"Hey," she said.

"Hey."

"Wanna come to Poetry Night?"

Of all the things Maya could have said, this was not what Tanner expected.

"What's Poetry Night?" He asked.

"At Pages and Pasta," Maya said. "They have a weekly Poetry Night every Tuesday—they've been doing it for like, decades. People read original poems, or sometimes just share poems they really like."

"Do I have to like poetry to go?" Tanner said.

Maya narrowed her eyes at him. "You don't have to but you should."

"Okay, do I have to *understand* poetry?"

Maya grinned. "No."

"Then let's go." Maya took his hand and led him towards the door.

They held hands as they crossed the street, but Maya discreetly dropped his when they walked into the bookstore cafe. Tables and shelves had been rearranged to create a small stage area along one wall, with chairs lined up in crowded rows. Tanner noticed Cosimo standing in a corner and lifted his hand in greeting, before sitting down in one of the chairs next to Maya. There were a few more faces that Tanner was beginning to recognize—people he had seen at the bar or the grocery store. Everyone was chatting, and Tanner got the sense that this was more of a community event than a tourist attraction.

A voice rang out through a microphone. Debbie stood on the raised platform and spoke. "Welcome to Poetry Night!" She said. "We have a few new faces here tonight…"

Debbie explained the way the night worked while Tanner stole a glance at Maya, who was watching Debbie and smiling. His eyes roamed over the piercings that lined her ear, the handful of necklaces she wore, her striking cheekbones. God, she was beautiful. The kind of beauty that made you stop in your tracks, that made your thoughts spin off-course. It wasn't "magazine beauty" necessarily… Maya's features were too strong for that. He just liked looking at her.

Maya turned her head and met his eyes. She smiled at him, a slow warmth spreading across her face. Tanner smiled back, and kept smiling even after Maya had turned her attention back to Debbie.

Tanner didn't dislike poetry, he just didn't always understand it. But he found he wasn't able to pay very close attention at first anyway…Maya had pressed her thigh against his and he felt it down the length of his entire body. He was aching to take her hand, to put his arm around her shoulder, to turn and whisper something in her ear—he didn't even know what, he just wanted closeness. But he took his cue from Maya having dropped his hand before entering Pages and Pasta, and tried to keep his focus on the words being spoken at the microphone.

A man named Kenny read a poem about fishing, and Maya's friend Anne read a poem about her baby getting older, after which Maya cheered loudly, the baby in question being held by a man standing behind the back row. After each new poem, the room erupted into applause, and Tanner felt it filling him up, all the love these people seemed to have for each other. He thought back to his conversation with Cosimo, about his sense that he could maybe belong here.

A little girl named Emily walked to the microphone and very solemnly read a poem she had written about sunsets, to the loudest applause of the night. And suddenly it was too much—too much goodness, too much belonging.

Tanner stopped clapping to press the heels of his hands into his eyes, waiting for the feelings in his chest to stop gripping him so tightly. But he felt like his lungs were being squeezed and he couldn't get his hands to stop feeling so shaky, so he stood up quickly and walked to the back of the room.

He placed one hand on his chest and tried to breathe normally. He saw Maya turn around and look at him questioningly. Tanner tried to smile but wasn't sure he succeeded, because Maya frowned in return and then stood up.

She walked to the door of the shop, then turned and looked at him. He followed her outside, then stood across from her in the chilly twilight.

Maya was looking at him with concern. "Are you okay?" She asked.

Tanner tried to find words to explain that all he'd ever wanted was a home and now that West Tindale was starting to feel like one, he was scared out of his mind. He opened his mouth to speak, then closed it again. His hand pressed into his chest again.

Maya watched all of this, and then held out her hand. "Come on," she said. "Let's go for a walk."

Tanner placed his hand in hers and followed her steps. She didn't speak, and he didn't try to either. They ambled past the Dairy Queen, the candy shop on their left, the knife shops and souvenir shops along Pine Ridge Avenue. Tanner shortened his stride the tiniest bit to allow Maya to keep up with him easily. They turned onto Outpost Way and had walked another two blocks before Tanner felt the grip in his chest beginning to loosen, his breath coming more easily.

He turned and looked at Maya. "Thanks," he said.

She met his eyes. "No problem." She paused as they kept walking. "Do you want to talk about it?" she asked.

Tanner thought for a moment. "I'm not sure…I don't know if I know how."

"You don't have to."

"No, I…I want to try. It's just that…West Tindale is starting to feel like home and even though that's what I want, it scares the shit out of me."

"The home part?" Maya asked.

Tanner thought for a moment. "The wanting part," he said. Maya stopped walking, and Tanner looked at her. Finally, she nodded.

"I know what you mean," she said. She took a deep breath. "Can I show you something?"

"Of course," Tanner said. Maya turned them onto 4th

Avenue, then again onto Tindale Way, heading back towards the bookstore cafe and the old schoolhouse. It was late enough that most of the shops were closed, the streets mostly empty. They'd almost made their way back to Pine Ridge when Maya stopped and turned them both towards a shop window.

It was a tiny shop, the window empty except for a "For Lease" sign. Maya stood looking at it for a long moment.

"What is this?" Tanner finally asked.

Maya took a deep breath. "It's where…if I had a soap shop, if I could make Tindale Soap Co. a full-time thing, this is where I would want it to be."

Tanner looked more closely at the vacant storefront. He could picture it—Maya setting up displays in the window, closing for half an hour to eat lunch at Pages and Pasta around the corner.

"I know it's silly," Maya said. "Soap isn't going to change the world or anything, and it's not even the soap itself, it's just the…it's doing something for myself."

"Have you talked to the real estate agent?"

Maya shook her head. "I'd have to talk to my parents first."

"Why don't you?"

Maya looked up at him. "Because even though it's for a different reason, I know what you mean about that feeling you were talking about. It's too much. The wanting part scares the shit out of me, too."

Tanner looked at Maya's full expressive eyes, the longing he saw in them. "You could if you—"

But Maya shook her head and held a hand up, cutting him off. She squeezed her eyes shut and gave her head another tiny shake.

Before he could even think about it, he pulled Maya into him and crushed her against his chest. He placed a kiss on the top of her head and heard her huff out a watery laugh.

"I'm supposed to be comforting you," she said, her voice muffled against his shirt.

"Maya," Tanner whispered, placing more kisses into her hair. "Maya." He didn't have other words to express what he was feeling, so he just said her name instead.

CHAPTER 19

Big News

MAYA

Maya didn't know what to expect when she decided to show Tanner the empty storefront. She was trying to think of a way to show him that she understood, that she knew what it felt like to want and be afraid of the wanting. But whatever she had envisioned, it wasn't crying into Tanner's chest while he whispered her name and left kisses all over her hair.

She tilted her face up to look at him, and when she met his eyes, they were so full of feeling that she didn't know what to say. But she didn't need to say anything. Tanner put his hands on either side of her face. His thumbs brushed her tears away, and after a brief moment of looking into her eyes, he leaned down to kiss her.

It was a slow, lingering kiss. The heat from their night in the alleyway still burned, but beneath it was now a tender ache that Maya felt deep in her bones. Warmth spread through her body as Tanner kissed her, his lips parting gently, his hands moving to tangle in her hair. He was all she could feel, all she could think, taking up so much space that there wasn't room for anyone or anything else.

"Tanner," Maya whispered between kisses.

"Maya," Tanner replied. Maya didn't have anything else she could say with words, so she changed the angle of her head to deepen their kiss. She heard Tanner's intake of breath, felt his body molding against hers. She felt a whimpering moan exit her chest, and suddenly Tanner's lips were moving with more hunger. Tanner spread his wide hands over her hips and she felt herself being pushed backward, until her back hit the window of the storefront.

Maya could feel Tanner growing hard against her as their lips moved together. His hands were pressing into her waist, her ribs, then over her breasts, cupping them roughly. Maya could hear her own breath growing ragged, feel the heat that was building quickly in her core. She couldn't remember the last time she wanted someone this badly.

Maya widened her stance as Tanner stepped into her, until his thighs were between her legs. Her hips tilted, seeking the friction her body was desperate for. Tanner reached down and grabbed the backs of Maya's thighs, then lifted her right off her feet, her back still pressed against the cool glass of the window. He buried his face in her neck, leaving hot kisses along her jaw, her throat.

"All right! Get it!" a distant voice yelled.

Maya froze, and felt Tanner go still against her. He looked up into her face.

"I literally forgot we were in public," Maya whispered.

Tanner let Maya down with a sigh. "Me, too," he said. The two of them glanced up the street, where a group of four men were watching them from half a block away. All four of them were laughing.

"Nothing to see here, guys," Tanner said, raising his

voice to reach their audience. The men turned away, still laughing.

Maya sighed. It could have been a lot worse, with those men. But still.

"You okay?" Tanner said. His hands were resting on her waist.

Maya laid her hands on his forearms. "Yeah. Nothing kills a lady boner like street harassment, though."

Tanner smiled. "I'm just happy to give you a boner at all," he said.

Maya burst into laughter. "That's the most beautiful thing anyone has ever said to me."

Tanner's smile widened, and he laughed softly as he stepped away from Maya. He held out his hand. "Can I walk you home?" he said.

"Sure," Maya replied, and she took his hand.

MAYA WOKE up the next morning feeling completely unsettled. She couldn't stop thinking about Tanner, his lips pressed against hers, his tongue working in her mouth. His hands on her hips. The outline of his hard cock, aching for her in his jeans. All of those memories made her feel like her blood was on fire.

But it was the memory of the moments before their make-out that made her stomach truly drop. His crushing embrace, the tenderness of his kisses, the way her name sounded in his quiet rumbling voice. His thumbs brushing her tears away.

Maya got ready without a single thought in her head but Tanner. She was still feeling slightly disoriented when she got downstairs to the hotel break room, where everyone was gathered for the weekly meeting. She closed her eyes and willed herself to focus. When she opened her eyes again, she took in the room.

Now that she was paying attention, it seemed to her that the room was more crowded than usual. She frowned. Devan sidled up to her and in a low voice, asked "What's Mom and Dad's lawyer doing here?" Maya glanced around the room, and sure enough, sitting in a corner in a blue suit was Sonya Applegate, their lawyer from Silver Falls.

"No idea," Maya whispered. "Maybe something to do with the old schoolhouse?" As she said it, Maya realized that she still hadn't made very much progress toward the goal of getting Tanner to sell them the building. But if she was being honest, it was difficult to think about anything but Tanner when she was with him.

Before Devan could respond, Bruce clapped his hands in rhythm. "Good morning, all in Hitchin' Post Hotel gang!"

Everyone clapped their hands in the same rhythm back and shouted the standard response. "Good morning, we're all the Hitchin' Post Hotel gang!"

"What's our goal?" Bruce shouted.

"Make 'em feel at home!" came the response.

"What's our goal?"

"Make 'em feel at home!"

"Say it one more time!"

"Our home is their home, we'll make 'em feel at home! Whoooo!" The chant ended with a cheer.

Maya, with every part of her soul, absolutely hated the company cheer. It was obnoxious at best and cult-y at worst. Her parents had started doing it when she was little, after they'd gone to some business development seminar. Something about "building company spirit." It made her want to vomit, and she refused to participate unless she absolutely had to. Usually she busied herself with tying her shoe or some other excuse.

Today, she and Devan half-heartedly joined in, rolling their eyes at each other afterwards.

"Okay, team!" Bruce said. "Today is a very special day. Not only is it May 15th, marking the official start of our summer season, but we also have a very important announcement to make." He glanced around the room.

"Some of you are just starting with our little family, and some of you have been with us for years," he said. "You've watched our kids grow up, and you've been a part of the Hitchin' Post Hotel Gang for almost as long as the hotel has existed. So that's why we wanted you all here with us today as we make this announcement."

Harriet stepped up to join her husband in front of the group. Bruce put his arm around her and turned back to the crowd. Something about it made Maya's stomach drop. This felt bigger than a "start of summer announcement," and she couldn't quite put her finger on why it made her so anxious.

"We are so proud of our little hotel," Harriet said. "Some of you know we're working on plans to add a restaurant, although it's still in the works." Harriet looked over at Maya and winked, and Maya's anxiety grew. "But there comes a time in every journey when it's time to hang up your hat. So this is Bruce and I's last summer here at the Hitchin' Post Hotel."

Maya froze.

Bruce squeezed Harriet's shoulders. "After this, we're retiring. We're officially turning ownership and management of the hotel over to our two kids, Maya and Devan, who we know will continue to run this place as the important part of the community that it's become." Bruce turned his eyes to Maya and Devan. "Kids, we know running a family business has its challenges, some that we're navigating right now. But we are so proud of you, and we're so happy that we could give you this gift."

The room broke out into applause, but all Maya could hear was a harsh kind of buzzing in her ears. She turned to Devan, and he had the same look of shock Maya was sure was also on her face. But people were turning towards them, clapping and cheering, so Maya quickly pasted a smile on her face and mouthed "thank you" to her dad.

Bruce and Harriet were both beaming. Maya could hardly stand to see the looks on their faces. In the back of her mind, she somehow always knew this day would come, but it had come so suddenly, without warning, and now that it was here, it was like a lead weight in her stomach.

She didn't want this.

That was all Maya could think as people applauded, as her parents smiled at her and Devan across the room. *I don't want this, I don't want this, I don't want this.*

But she didn't have time to process any of those thoughts. She didn't have time to think about the half-formed vision of her soap shop disappearing from her future. She didn't have time to think about Devan's look of shock, or the want list she'd just barely made.

Everyone was watching, so Maya did what she always did when her parents wanted something from her. She smiled and handed it over.

CHAPTER 20

The Couch

TANNER

Okay, so Tanner Sullivan may have broken up with his longtime girlfriend (or long-time "person he was dating") roughly four seconds ago, but he officially, absolutely, and definitely had feelings for Maya Clark. His dick certainly did. Ever since their time in the alleyway that night, Tanner's thoughts of Maya had gone into overdrive.

The second he got home after Poetry Night, he did the same thing he'd done every night since the alleyway. He'd unzipped his jeans, laying down in his new bed and pumping his still-hard cock to thoughts of Maya until he felt a rush of relief. And still, all he wanted was to have her in his bed, under him, over him, beside him…really any position would do. There had been moments that first night when she had rolled her hips against him, against the thick muscles of his thigh, and he was ready to half-squat against a wall for the rest of his life, just in case Maya might want to grind on any part of him ever again.

After the tenderness and heat of their kisses after Poetry Night, and after Tanner had fucked his hand until he could think straight again, he laid on top of the covers and stared at the ceiling, his limbs spread out across the mattress. The bed was truly too big for this room, the heavy dark wood leaving only a few feet of space on either side. But he liked it anyway—the tall posts at each corner, the leaves carved into the headboard. He had found a used nightstand a few days earlier, and had emptied one of his boxes into the drawers. Chapstick, an old phone charger, a handful of condoms. The condoms gave him pause. He thought about throwing them away, but decided to keep them. *Just in case*, he told himself.

Later that evening, as he unpacked some of the furniture that had arrived at the old schoolhouse, Tanner kept wondering if he should call Maya. Or, you know, ask for her number so that he could call her. He was also wondering if what had happened between them (twice now) would happen again. He sure as hell hoped it would. He had more things he wanted to do to her. Or with her. Or both.

Tanner unwrapped the large gray couch he had ordered for the coffee house. He had seen it in Silver Falls, when he drove down a few days after buying the building. He was afraid it would be too big—it could easily seat four people. But now that it was in the high-ceilinged room, and he could see it against the dark blue walls and yellow curtains, it fit perfectly. The shape and pattern of it reminded Tanner a little bit of a seashell, with its curved back, divided into sections. One side was higher than the other, and the legs were a rich, dark wood that reached up in curled patterns onto the arms.

Tanner stepped back and smiled at the couch. Then he pulled out a new drop cloth and covered the fabric to protect it while he kept working. He was in the middle of unpacking a set of bookshelves to assemble when the door flew open.

Tanner looked up in alarm, and was shocked to see Maya slamming the door behind her as she stormed towards him. It was the end of the workday, and she was wearing a simple yellow dress that swished as she walked. By instinct, he took a step backward, but she grabbed the front of his shirt and pulled him towards her.

"Kiss me," she whispered, with a fierce desperation that set his blood on fire. He didn't need to be told twice. He grabbed her upper arms and practically lifted her off her feet as he pressed his lips to hers. Tanner was vaguely aware of both of them making noises of longing, Tanner's tongue exploring Maya's mouth, and her lips parting for him in response. His hands ran up along her ribs until one of her breasts was pressed firmly in his palm, and he could feel her clutching at his shirt.

"Wait—" Tanner tried to say, but it took him a few attempts to get the word out. He finally pushed Maya away long enough to say, "Give me one second," then he turned and began walking the perimeter of the room, closing curtains as he went. If he and Maya were about to tear each other's clothes off (which he hoped they were), he wanted privacy.

When he turned back to Maya, she was sitting on the new couch, her hands beneath her thighs. She was staring at the floor with a hint of a grimace across her face.

"What is it?" Tanner asked. Maya looked up at him, and for a second, he couldn't quite breathe. She was so fucking beautiful. Her brown hair falling in soft waves around her face and shoulders. But her eyes were looking at him with such feeling that he reached up and put a hand over his heart before he could even figure out why. The look on her face filled him with an ache he didn't even want to name.

"Are you okay?" he finally asked again.

Maya looked back down at the ground. Then she slowly shook her head. Tanner took a slow step forward, and when Maya didn't turn away, he closed the distance between them and lowered himself onto the couch beside her.

"Do you want to talk about it?" he asked softly.

Maya took a moment to answer. "My parents are retiring," she said.

Tanner wasn't quite sure if that was the entire story, so when Maya didn't say anything else, he said tentatively, "Congratulations to them?"

"No," Maya shook her head. "They're giving the hotel to me and Devan. After this summer. This is the last summer they're working at the hotel, and then it's all Devan and me. They announced it this morning." She looked up at him. "I…"

Tanner gazed back at her. What was he supposed to do when she looked at him like that? All vulnerable and strong and beautiful? He was pretty sure that he'd do almost anything she asked him to in this moment. She'd awoken something in him (again?)…some growling, protective thing that wanted to wrap her up and hold her forever.

As Maya looked at him, her eyes grew watery. She turned away and swiped angrily at her tears.

"Maya?" Tanner asked.

She turned back to him. "I don't want to run the hotel," she said in a small voice.

"Then don't," Tanner said.

"I don't know how not to."

"Have you ever told your parents what you want?"

Maya looked down, then shook her head. "You make it sound so easy," she said. "Like there aren't decades worth of expectations and hurt and disappointment and hope behind every sentence anyone speaks to anyone else in their family."

Tanner wasn't sure how to answer that. On the one hand, he did know how everything you said to the people you grew up with could be loaded with meaning. On the other hand, he had stopped giving a shit about what Len thought a long time before he'd died, and that had made it a helluva lot easier for Tanner to say whatever he wanted.

"I don't mean to make it sound easy," Tanner said. "It takes practice. You have to—"

"Could you be quiet for a minute?"

Tanner leaned back, then slowly laid his arm over the back of the couch—not quite encircling Maya, but there if she wanted to lean into him. He sat in silence, glancing at her now and then as she looked straight in front of her, working something out in her mind. They sat like that for at least five full minutes.

Eventually, Maya turned to face him, his arm still stretched out over the back of the couch.

"Can I...?" Maya started. Tanner watched her close her eyes and take a deep breath. "I want to...I want to do this." She lifted herself up, then moved one leg over his body until she was straddling him. She settled down onto his lap, and he placed his hands on her hips.

"God, *please* do this," Tanner replied. Maya smiled, then leaned forward and kissed him. It was a question at first, but as he kissed her back, her lips moved with more certainty.

He ran his palms up her body, from her thigh, over her hips, across her ribs. His hips rolled up into her, some fierce need he could barely control taking over his body. The sound Maya made at his movement made it difficult to think anything coherent.

His fingers ran back down and brushed over the hem of Maya's dress and he looked up into her face.

"I want to take this off," he said. "Can I take this off?"

When Maya nodded, he lifted her dress up over her head. He was face to face with her bra, her perfect tits filling the lace cups. He drew his hands up to them, and they were full and so soft in his hands. He watched Maya's face as he kneaded them, gently at first, and then with a firmer hand. Her head had fallen back and her eyes were closed, and when he massaged her more deeply, she bit her lip with a whimper, then leaned forward to kiss his lips.

Tanner loved the way she felt on top of him, loved the feeling of her bare thighs on either side of his legs, the weight of her. He loved the lacy underwear he could feel under his hands. He was sure it looked incredible, but getting a good look at it meant pushing Maya off his lap, and he absolutely did not want to do that at the moment.

Slowly, Maya reached between them and unbuttoned his jeans, easing the zipper down so she could reach inside and run her hand up and down his hard length, over his briefs. Tanner moaned at her touch. "Jesus," he gritted it out. They weren't even skin-to-skin, and he wasn't sure how much longer he could last like this.

When Maya took her hand away, Tanner opened his eyes to find her reaching behind herself to unhook her bra and pull it off her shoulders. And then her breasts were bare, the points hard in front of him.

"Oh my god," Tanner said quietly. He could feel his cock twitch, an ache that was growing stronger by the second. He leaned forward and pressed his lips to one of the pink buds in front of him. He opened his mouth and let his tongue roll in slow circles around her nipple, hearing Maya hiss out her pleasure at the sensation. He turned to her other breast to give it the same treatment, then spread his hands wide over her ribs, kissing every part of her he could reach. Soon, his hips were tilting upwards with more insistence, desperate for more friction between his and Maya's bodies.

"Tell me to fuck you," he whispered, hearing the rough desperation in his voice.

Maya's breathing sped up.

"God, I want to fuck you," Tanner continued, his face buried in Maya's neck. "It's all I've been thinking about. For days. Weeks."

Maya reached a hand up and tangled her fist into his hair.

"I want…" she whispered, breathless.

"Tell me," Tanner replied, running his mouth over her breasts, her neck, her collarbones.

"I want you to…" Maya spoke between gasps, "make me come…with your tongue."

Tanner smiled and lifted his head, surprised to see some uncertainty in Maya's face.

"Yeah?" he said.

Maya grinned and nodded. She glanced down at Tanner's lap, his opened jeans and the outline of his erect cock beneath his briefs. She looked up at his face again.

"The way you showed me you would. In the alleyway." Maya pulled one of Tanner's fingers into her mouth and gently sucked on it. Tanner thought he might explode.

"I…want to make you come with my tongue," Tanner said. He lifted her off his lap and set her down on the couch.

"Is the drop cloth okay?" he asked, glancing at the fabric spread out under them. "Is it too scratchy?"

"It's fine, please just hurry," Maya replied.

Tanner grinned. He knelt in front of her and pulled her legs towards him. He was right about the underwear.

She looked incredible. He stopped for a moment and just looked at her, the swell of her breasts, the dip of her waist. The soft skin around her belly button. The spread of her ass and thighs on the couch. What was that part of a woman called, that thick beautiful place near their hips? He wanted to grab Maya there and push himself into her. But first, he wanted to taste her.

CHAPTER 21

The Bed

MAYA

Maya didn't think anyone had ever looked at her body like Tanner was right now. Like she was a feast and he was starving. She felt a rush of heat between her legs and squirmed slightly with impatience. Tanner caught her eye and smiled wickedly. Then he reached forward to hook his fingers into the sides of her panties, and she lifted her hips so that he could pull them down and sit back on his heels.

The air was cold on her bare skin, but she glanced down at Tanner and then he was all she could think about. Tanner kneeling in front of her, his shirt still on, his pants undone, his hair messy. His face inches away from where she wanted him. She felt another rush of wetness and tilted her hips up involuntarily, spreading her legs even further. But Tanner was taking his time. He inched himself forward, running his hands along the outside of her legs. He lifted one of her legs over his shoulder, then the other. He brought his mouth closer and whispered, "I've been thinking about this for a long time." Maya gasped at the hot breath of his words against her skin. "I've been wanting to taste you…" Tanner continued, letting his lips brush against her folds. "I've been wanting to feel you on my tongue…"

Maya felt the heat of Tanner's mouth hover gently over her clit, and she tightened her legs briefly around his head, reaching down to grab a handful of his hair.

"More," she whispered.

And then Tanner gave her more.

He used his mouth like she was a beautiful puzzle that he was solving. If something made her spasm with pleasure, he did it again. If she didn't respond as strongly to something, he tried something else. He moved slow, then fast, hard, then soft. He worked steadily, his soft beard brushing against her skin, his tongue and lips and fingers sending her to higher and higher heights. She could feel her pleasure building, warm and sweet and liquid in her core.

He reached up and clutched one of her breasts, settling into a perfect rhythm with his tongue. Maya looked down to see him watching her, his mouth open wide, his other hand resting on her lower belly, his thumb on her clit. The sight of him shot fire through Maya's veins, and she felt the beginnings of what she longed for.

"Tanner, I'm—"

Tanner licked steadily, not changing a thing about what he was doing, and within seconds, Maya's orgasm came crashing through her. It was strong enough to make her cry out, her knees lifting, her thighs squeezing until the waves subsided. Tanner's mouth didn't leave the spot between her legs until she was limp with satisfaction.

Finally, Maya laid back, spent with pleasure, her legs relaxed on Tanner's shoulders. Once her breathing was back to normal, she sat up and looked down at Tanner, his beard slick with her sex. He was smiling at her with a gleam in his eye, rubbing his neck with one hand.

"Did I…did I hurt you?" Maya asked. She realized that she had sort of crushed his skull a little bit in the heat of the moment.

"Nope," Tanner said. "And even if you had, what a way to be injured."

Maya laughed and laid her head back. "Good lord," she whispered. Tanner crawled up to sit next to her. He ran one hand down her body, from her throat to the beginnings of the hair between her legs, a gentle act of adoration.

"You are fucking stunning," he said.

Maya glanced at the front of Tanner's open pants, his erection still pressing against his briefs.

"Do you want me to…?" she asked.

Tanner just raised his eyebrows at her.

"I can, you know, return the favor. With my mouth, I mean," Maya added, reaching toward Tanner's open fly. Tanner caught her wrist and she looked up at his face.

"Do you *want* to return the favor?"

Maya shrugged. "It's only fair," she said. What she *really* wanted was to get dressed, then go with Tanner to somewhere with a bed. She wanted to pull his clothes off and run her hands along his body and then ride him until he couldn't walk. Which they could do on this couch. But a bed would be better.

"Maya," Tanner said, still holding her wrist. "A shrug is not exactly…I don't want a blow job if you don't want to give me one. Do you…like to give blow jobs?"

Maya thought for a moment. "It depends," she said.

Tanner let go of her wrist and settled further into the couch. "On what?" he asked.

"I guess on the person," Maya said. "There are things I like about blow jobs and things I don't."

"Such as…?"

Maya paused. She wasn't sure how to answer, so she leaned over to grab her clothes to stall for time. She pulled her dress over her head, then said, "I like making someone else feel really good. I like…connecting the intimacy of my mouth with the intimacy of what someone has between their legs. If that makes sense. But I don't like choking, or when someone is like, forcing themselves into my mouth. And I don't like it when a guy comes in my mouth." She paused, then grinned and added, "Girls can come in my mouth, though."

Maya watched Tanner swallow hard, then nod. "Noted," he said. "Next question: do you want to have sex with me?"

Maya looked at him. "What did we just do?"

"Oh, uh," Tanner stumbled a little.

"Do you think it's only sex if your penis is involved?" Maya said.

Tanner was quiet. "That is a very good point," he said, looking at the floor. "Okay, new question," he said, looking at her from under the curls falling onto his forehead. When he spoke, Maya felt it in her core. "Do you want me to put my dick in you? Do you want me to fuck your perfect pussy with my cock?"

Maya stopped breathing. When she looked back up at Tanner, his hair messy, his lips still wet, his eyes piercing hers.

"I want to go to your place," she said.

Tanner's hands were tight on the steering wheel of his truck. Maya stole a glance at his profile. His head nearly touched the roof of the cabin. When he had told her where he lived, she suggested they walk, but he had grabbed her hand and said, "Not fast enough." It took all of two minutes to drive to Tanner's apartment, but when they pulled in, Tanner turned the engine off and just sat there, looking out the front window. He leaned his elbow on the driver side door and bit one of his nails.

"Is everything okay?" Maya finally asked.

Tanner took a deep breath, then turned to her. "Yeah," he said, smiling.

When he opened his front door and led her inside, Maya kicked her shoes off and then stood for a moment, looking around.

"You have…no furniture," she said.

She felt Tanner standing behind her and she turned to look at him. God, it was fun how tall he was. She loved craning her neck to see his face. He reached up and rubbed the back of his neck.

"Yeah," he said slowly. "I've been uh…I've been focused on the old schoolhouse."

Maya felt something in her stomach hitch slightly. Like she had been walking downstairs and missed a step. She suddenly thought of her parents, smiling at her and Devan in the hotel lobby earlier, of the way they'd told her she had "carte blanche" to get the old schoolhouse back.

But tonight wasn't for them. Tonight was for her.

She smiled up at Tanner. "Do you at least have a bed?"

He grinned. "Do I ever," he replied. "Hold on." He kicked his shoes and socks off, then crouched and grabbed Maya around the waist, lifting her up and starting toward what she assumed was the bedroom. She hooked her ankles into the small of his back and leaned in to kiss his neck. When he moaned and stopped walking, she looked up.

"I can't walk when you're doing that," he said. She grinned and leaned in to whisper into his ear.

"Then hurry and get me to your bed so I can keep doing it," she said softly. In a few steps, she felt herself being lowered down and she glanced around her.

"You weren't kidding," she said. "This is some bed."

Tanner stood looking down at her, and then he leaned forward and placed his hands on either side of her. "What do you want?" he said quietly.

"I want to take your shirt off," Maya said.

Tanner nodded. Maya reached up and began undoing his buttons, surprised to find her hands trembling slightly. She pushed his open shirt down over his shoulders and ran her hands across his broad chest, then down over his stomach, tracing the curls of hair down towards the top of his pants. When she looked up at Tanner, his eyes were closed. She reached up to his shirt again, tugging it farther down his arms, but it got stuck at his wrists.

"Off," she said, starting to laugh. "I want this off."

Tanner laughed and pulled his arms all the way free. "What else do you want?" he said.

Maya scooted backward onto the bed, then lifted her dress over her head, tossing it aside. She hadn't bothered to put her bra and panties back on at the old schoolhouse, so her naked body rested against Tanner's sheets. "I want you on top of me."

Tanner knelt on the bed and started to crawl towards her.

"Wait!" Maya said.

Tanner froze, a look of nervousness suddenly crossing his face.

"Sorry," Maya said, smiling. "I want…take your pants off, too."

Tanner's face split into a grin, and he rolled over onto his back.

"Wait!" Maya said again.

"What?" Tanner was looking vaguely panicked again.

"I want to do it."

Tanner slowly lowered his head onto the pillow, and placed his hands behind his head. He looked up at Maya, then glanced down towards his jeans, smirking.

Maya bit her lip to hold back a grin. She rolled so that she was straddling him and kissed him long and hard, before scooting down and making quick work of his pants. After throwing them onto the floor, she reached up to run her hands along the sides of his thighs.

There was just so much of him. The girth of his legs, the width of his hips. This is what people were talking about when they said someone was "barrel-chested." She kept running her hands over him. But Maya's focus was quickly drawn to the growing bulge between Tanner's legs. She laid a hand over the warm cotton of his briefs, feeling his arousal. Reaching inside, she slowly ran one finger up its length, from the base to where it was pointed upwards near the waistband of his briefs. When she got to the tip, Tanner gasped and sucked his stomach in suddenly.

Maya drew her hand away, startled. "Sorry," she said. "I didn't—"

Tanner grabbed her wrist. "That felt so fucking good," he said. Maya grinned, then reached down to do it again. When she slipped her fingers into his waistband, she watched his hips buck gently, then she slowly tugged at his briefs until he was free. She slid them down his legs and then made her way back up his body.

She had intended to take her time, but seeing him hard

and aching for her suddenly made her desperate. She needed to feel him inside of her, as soon as possible.

"Condom?" she said, her voice coming out as a fierce whisper. She rolled off of him so that Tanner could reach over and open his dresser drawer. He rolled the condom on in a matter of seconds, then turned and looked at her, his eyes more heated than she had ever seen them.

CHAPTER 22

More of This

TANNER

Maya's hair was messy around her face, her cheeks flushed, her skin warm in the soft light of his room. Tanner involuntarily let out a moan from the back of his throat and Maya bit her lip to hold back a smile.

He rolled over her, holding himself above her, then settled himself between her thighs. He leaned down to kiss along her perfect jawline. He couldn't quite get himself to believe this was happening. But Maya's fingers were in his hair, her nails raking over his scalp, and her breasts were pressed against his bare chest, and she was wrapping her legs around his waist. Even just that touch between their bodies felt incredible. His lips moved back up to find hers, one hand cupping the back of her head, angling to kiss her more deeply.

Tanner felt Maya's hips tilt upwards once, then again. He reached a hand down between them, finding her most sensitive spot and rubbing back and forth with his fingers until she was practically writhing beneath him.

"Tanner," she whispered between kisses. "If you don't..."

He raised himself above her to smile into her face. "Did you want me to do something…?"

Maya stared hard at him, all heat and longing, then reached down between their bodies to grasp him firmly in her hand. She positioned the tip of him against the wet heat between her legs. Tanner sucked in a breath.

"I want you to fuck me," she said, widening her legs.

Tanner took a breath, then pushed into her. Maya arched her back and reached behind her with one hand to steady herself on the headboard. Tanner slid slowly out of her, then back in, trying to control himself.

Maya reached up and grasped the back of his neck. "More," she whispered.

Tanner looked into her face for a moment, then drove into her with more force. He loved hearing her gasp. He wanted to coax more of those sounds out of her, wanted to fill her with pleasure. He pumped his hips harder, and Maya's cries got louder.

"God," he whispered. "I love hearing you." Maya looked up at him, biting her lip, then held her gaze as he drove into her again, letting out another one of those incredible sounds.

Heat was building in him, pushing him closer to the edge, but he was determined to bring Maya with him. He reached down and began moving his fingers against her clit again, and within minutes he felt Maya beginning to shudder. Her walls tightened around him as she cried out, her legs shaking as she rode through her climax.

He slowed his movement as Maya's breathing deepened and her moans softened.

"Fucking god," she whispered. After a moment, she looked up at him. "I want to be on top," she said.

Tanner grinned, then rolled off of her. Maya turned and straddled his thighs, then slowly scooted forward until she was right above where he wanted her. Then she reached between their bodies, positioned him where she wanted and sank down, inch by slow, agonizingly perfect inch. When she started moving, Tanner reached up and caught both of Maya's hands in his. He laced their fingers together, resting his elbows on the mattress to let her use his arms for leverage. She pressed her palms against his and ground into him. This time, Tanner was the one who couldn't keep quiet. He heard himself moaning, his voice mixing with Maya's. Looking up, he didn't think he'd ever seen anything more beautiful in his life. Maya's eyes were closed in pleasure, her breasts bouncing slightly as she rode him.

He wasn't sure how much longer he could last like this. "Honey," he whispered. "I'm getting close. Do you want me to…?" Maya looked down at him, smiled, then untangled one of her hands from his so that she could lean forward and rest it on his chest.

"I want to watch you come," she said. It was all Tanner needed to hear. She sped up her movements, and Tanner reached up a free hand and clutched one of her breasts. One more second, two more, and suddenly his release took over him, wave after wave of it.

When his breathing had slowed enough for him to think straight, Maya slowly climbed off of him and laid down, her head on his chest. Their bodies were slick with sweat, and Tanner ran one hand idly up and down Maya's back.

"You," he said quietly, "are so…fucking…I don't even know…hot."

Tanner had meant to be more articulate, but he was too blissed out to think straight. Maya laughed. "I know," she said. She turned her head to look up into his face. "It's hot when other people recognize it."

"Oh, I recognize it."

"Your DICK recognizes it!" Maya replied, and Tanner burst into laughter. His laughter made Maya laugh, and they lay in bed, laughing until they could hardly breathe.

～

AFTER CLEANING UP, Maya sat up in the bed. "I'm starving," she said.

"What time is it?"

Maya reached for her phone, then turned it over. "1 am?"

"Definitely too late for anything from in town. I think I have a frozen pizza?"

Maya grinned at him. "You already got me into bed. You don't have to keep seducing me."

"If I had known that was all it would take," Tanner laughed. He got up and stood naked in the kitchen, putting the pizza in the oven. Afterward, they ate cross-legged in the bed, their clothes still strewn on the ground around them.

"Why don't you have any furniture?" Maya asked, tilting her head to catch the cheese that was dripping off her slice of pizza.

Tanner watched her lips, hypnotized, before mentally shaking himself. "I have this bed," he replied.

"Yeah you do," Maya grinned slyly. "But it's literally one of like, two pieces of furniture you have."

"I've just been focused on the old schoolhouse," he said, then immediately regretted it. He and Maya sat in silence for a few moments, the specter of the old schoolhouse floating between them. Finally, Maya set her pizza aside and stood up. She walked out of the room, and a few moments later, Tanner heard the bathroom sink running.

When she sauntered back in, her naked body practically glowing in the light, Tanner sat up.

"Sorry," he said. "I know the old schoolhouse is—"

Maya cut him off. "I don't want to talk about the old schoolhouse," she said. She crawled onto the bed, then reached between his legs, cupping him gently. She leaned forward over him, her hair brushing against his chest as she whispered, "I want more of this."

WHEN TANNER WOKE up the next morning, slow and languid in the early light, he lay in his bed in disbelief. A smile spread across his face as he remembered Maya's gaze, her hands working him until he thought he would explode. Flashes of the night before played themselves out in his mind—Maya's frantic cries, his own hands grasping her hips, and later when he had to grip the headboard with both hands to steady himself as he pumped into her, something wild and desperate in the movement of their hips. In the morning light, he turned to wrap himself around her, but opened his eyes to find that he was the only one tangled in the bedding.

He raised his head, listening for movement elsewhere in the apartment. "Maya?" He called out.

Silence. He fell back against the pillows. She was probably at work. He hoped she was at work...that she hadn't just panicked and left. She did have the kind of job you had to show up for in the morning—unlike his, where he could just show up when he wanted to. When he turned to grab his phone from the nightstand, he found a note there. Maya's name and phone number, and a command: "text me."

He thumbed out a quick message.

This is Tanner and you're so fucking I don't know…hot.

Maya answered right away.

Your dick recognizes it

Tanner grinned throughout his entire morning routine, the whole walk to the old schoolhouse, and through the first hour of work. His grin had widened when he walked in and saw the drop-cloth-covered couch, remembered Maya's naked body arching with pleasure at his head between her legs. He kept glancing over at the hotel next door, thinking about running over there, grabbing Maya's waist, kissing her breathless.

When his phone rang around noon, he almost dropped it in his eagerness to answer. But it wasn't Maya's number on the screen.

When he answered, the familiar automated voice told him he had a call from California State Prison Solano.

"Hey Billy," he said.

"Hey fucker," Billy's voice said. "How's it going, man?"

"Good," Tanner replied. "Really good."

"Dude, I can hear your grin from here. Did Camille finally come visit?"

"Uhhh…"

"What the hell does that mean?"

"Um…Camille broke up with me."

"What? When?"

"Like, a week ago?" Tanner sat down on the couch. "Over the phone, which sucked, but it's actually…fine?"

Tanner told Billy about Camille not calling him her boyfriend, about how none of it was working, and about how Tanner didn't feel good about the whole "not her boyfriend" thing, but that ultimately, he knew it was the right thing for them to break up.

"So how come you're doing 'really good'?" Billy asked, after commiserating.

Tanner debated with himself for a minute. "There's this girl…"

"Damn, son!"

"I don't even really know what this is, like, what we are," Tanner said, "But she spent the night last night and she's…she's kind of incredible."

"Congrats, man," Billy said.

Tanner kept smiling as he worked, and he and Billy talked until Billy had to leave for dinner.

CHAPTER 23

The Argument

MAYA

Maya spent the entirety of the day replaying images from the night before. How could someone be so absurdly hot? With his hands and his mouth and his shoulders and his dick and his eyes? At the front desk during her shift, Maya made roughly two hundred mistakes, and kept checking her phone for messages from Tanner. She could hear him working next door, and the sounds of construction were somehow turning her on so much she could barely function. He sent her a handful of texts throughout the day, telling her how he couldn't stop thinking about her, telling her he was thinking of specific moments from the night before. Maya could hardly contain her grin with every reply she sent. She asked to see him after her shift was over. He told her to come over to the old schoolhouse.

At the edges of her mind, she kept feeling a question bumping around. A "what are you doing with Tanner Sullivan?" A wondering what last night meant, and what was going to happen next. But she didn't want to think about that just yet, so she batted the question away. She'd answer it later, after she'd had her way with him a few more times. She grinned to herself at the thought.

When Maya finally walked upstairs towards her room at the end of the day, she heard Devan arguing with their parents. She rolled her eyes and sighed. She wondered if other families fought this way—petty arguments over stupid things, where everyone was furious with everyone else for a day and then got over it. The door to her parents' room was open and she could hear their raised voices.

Then she caught some of what Devan was actually saying, and paused when she got to her bedroom door to listen more closely.

"You never asked! You never fucking asked!"

Maya frowned. Devan never swore in front of their parents. He was probably upset about scheduling, but the swearing was new. Their parents often switched their kids' schedules around, assuming that they'd be more accommodating than the other hotel employees. Which, Maya admitted, was very annoying, but not quite "f-bomb in front of your parents" annoying.

"Devan, don't use that language in front of your mother," Bruce said.

"Then don't rearrange my entire life without talking to me about it first! Or Maya's!"

"Maya is grateful," Harriett said. Maya's frown deepened at the mention of her name.

"How do you know? Huh?" Devan shouted. "How do you fucking know? Have you ever asked either of us if this is what we want to do with our lives?"

Maya tiptoed down the hallway towards her parents' room. This sounded like more than a scheduling argument.

"We've planned this since you were children," Harriett said. "We're handing over a successful—"

"Oh, *successful?!*" Devan replied. "Then why are you so damn desperate for another revenue stream? You're handing us a sinking ship and acting like it's the greatest fucking gift on earth!"

"Stop yelling!" Bruce said.

"The hell I won't," Devan replied. There was a long pause, and then Maya heard Devan say something like "I can't do this shit anymore." In seconds, he was storming out of the room, passing Maya forcefully. "I'm going to Silver Falls. Don't call me."

"Devan?" Maya called after him, then followed him partway down the stairs. "Devan!"

Devan stopped, then turned and looked up to face Maya. "I'm sorry, I can't," he said. "I'll call you later, but I've got to get out of here." He turned and took the rest of the stairs two at a time. Maya turned around and walked back up to her parents' room. She found Harriett crying, Bruce's arms around her. When Harriett saw Maya standing in the doorway, she burst into fresh sobs and reached her arms out.

Maya's stomach filled with dread. She hated feeling like she was choosing sides. But she didn't want to ignore her mother. She stepped into the room and hugged Harriett. After a few moments, her mom looked up at her and said, "It's a gift. The hotel is a gift. For you and Devan. We spent decades working for it and your brother doesn't want it."

The lead in Maya's stomach hardened. "Did he say that?"

Bruce spoke. "He just told us that he's quitting...that he doesn't want the hotel, now or ever."

Maya felt a crack split down her middle. Devan did what she had wanted to do, and part of her was proud of him for it. For finally speaking up for himself and what he wanted. Maya longed to do the same thing, with almost everything in her. And maybe now would be the best moment—she could clear up any expectations and get the hurt all over with at once. But she looked at her parents, at her father's weary eyes, at her mother's tear-stained face, and she just…couldn't. They would never speak to her again if she abandoned them. If she took the gift of the hotel and handed it back to them.

"Honey, you understand what we're trying to give you," Harriett said. "We're counting on you. We want this hotel to stay in the family. We've dreamed of having a plaque in the lobby, talking about how this business has been in the family for generations. You're the next generation. You and Devan. If Devan won't carry it on, you have to. For us. For the Clarks."

Maya felt like she might throw up, but she nodded her head.

"I won't let you down," she said.

Fifteen minutes later, Maya told her parents she was going for a walk. Which was sort of true—she did have to walk to get to the old schoolhouse. She didn't even bother changing her clothes. She just needed to see Tanner. When she opened the door, there was a moment before Tanner noticed her, when she just watched him. His broad shoulders inside his t-shirt, the way his jeans hugged him. She smiled in spite of herself. He turned around and caught her eye.

"Hey," he said.

Suddenly, she felt like bursting into tears. She walked forward and laid her head on his chest. He reached up and ran a hand gently over her hair.

"Hey," he said again, more quietly this time.

Maya thought about how to answer. "I don't know how to do this," she whispered.

"Which this?" Tanner asked. "Us this?"

Maya shook her head. That question *did* need answering, but she could only handle one large question at a time.

"My parents. The hotel." Maya looked up at Tanner. He was gazing down on her with such tenderness, such care, that Maya could hardly stand it. She lowered her head to his chest again and explained about the fight between Devan and her parents, about how she'd promised again to carry on their legacy, despite the awful pit in her stomach.

Tanner took Maya's face in his hands and tilted her gaze upwards towards him.

"Maya, sweetheart," Tanner said. "What do you want?"

"I want you to kiss me."

He leaned down and pressed his lips gently to hers, then pulled away and looked into her face again. "What else do you want? Really truly want?"

Maya shook her head. "I don't…maybe to own the soap shop? No, definitely to own the soap shop. But it feels…impossible. I just know what I don't want. I don't want to run the hotel. I don't want to spend my entire life working at that hotel."

Tanner took her hand and led her to the couch. He sat them both down and put his arm around her. "Come here," he said softly. Maya melted into him. She allowed her head to rest on his chest, felt his hand drawing gentle lines up and down her back. He turned and placed a kiss on the top of her head.

This, Maya thought. *I want this.*

She turned and placed a kiss on Tanner's neck, and

despite her despair, she was thrilled to discover his breathing speeding up, his heart beating strong in his chest. She tilted her head and kissed down his throat, then back up his jaw. Tanner let out a little noise of pleasure, so Maya turned and straddled his lap, taking his face in her hands to kiss his lips. His hands drew slowly up her sides, then down her back until they were cupping her ass and pulling her more deeply into him.

She broke their kiss and whispered, "I want *you*."

Tanner pressed his face into her neck, his chin grazing the tops of her breasts. "I want *you*," he whispered. "All the time." He drew his nose in a long slow line down the column of her neck, nudging the collar of her work shirt open, planting slow kisses along her skin. Maya felt her blood rush, an ache in her chest and between her legs. She could feel Tanner growing hard beneath her.

"I want you on top of me," Tanner whispered into her skin. "I want you under me, taking all of me into you." Maya bit her lip, need building in her, her breath beginning to come in gasps. He reached out and grasped her wrist, then pushed her hand down between their bodies to the front of his jeans. "Do you feel what you do to me?" he whispered. Maya felt her blood rush, deepening the ache in between her legs.

A voice startled both of them. "Hello! Oh my—" Maya turned to the front door and saw, with absolute horror, her mother.

She jumped off Tanner's lap and stood up. "Mom! What the hell!?"

Harriett had turned to the side, covering her face with one hand while she replied. "I just…your dad and I saw you come over here and…"

Maya felt frozen in place. Tanner was still seated on the couch, and she realized with a fresh wave of embarrassment that he probably couldn't stand without revealing his hard-on, which just added to the nightmare. Maya's chest felt tight with panic.

"Mom, why would—why did you follow me?"

"Well, you really took that 'blank check' thing to heart, didn't you?" Harriett said, smiling slyly at her daughter.

"Harriett?" Bruce stepped in behind his wife. "What's going on?"

"Maya definitely got our hint," Harriett said, giggling.

Maya felt her stomach drop, and she glanced over at Tanner, who was looking at everyone with a slightly confused look on his face. Her heart was thudding in her chest, and that frozen feeling inside of her was growing even stronger, like she couldn't think straight. Tanner finally met Maya's eyes.

"Maya?" he asked.

CHAPTER 24

Blank Check

TANNER

Tanner was having a hard time processing the many things that were taking place at the moment. This isn't how he pictured meeting Maya's parents, for one thing, but something about what Maya's mother had just said was snagging in his brain.

"What hint?" Tanner asked.

Before she could answer, Maya's mom spoke again, a giggle still evident in her voice. "Took the hint and *ran* with it."

Tanner sought out Maya's eyes again. Any arousal he had experienced before had evaporated in the light of the current situation. He stood up.

"Maya?" He asked again. "What is she talking about?"

Maya closed her eyes, then covered her face with her hands. Her breath was short and panicked. Tanner took a step forward and placed his hands gently on the sides of her arms. "Hey," he said quietly.

"This is a nightmare," Maya said through her hands.

"It's okay," Tanner said. "I just…can you tell me what your mom meant? About…" Tanner almost didn't want to finish the sentence, dread settling in his stomach. "You… taking a hint? And running with it?"

"Are you *actually* dating this man, Maya?" This was from the man Tanner assumed was Maya's father. His voice was laced with disappointment. "Because we didn't mean for you to take it *that* far. You just needed to get the old schoolhouse, not a boyfriend."

Maya uncovered her face and looked over at her father, her eyes filled with pain. "Dad," she said.

"Oh, come on, Bruce," Harriet said, swatting her husband's arm playfully. "It's the oldest move in the book." Harriet winked at Maya.

Tanner had no idea what Maya would say to her parents calling him her boyfriend. This was not how he had planned for them to have this conversation. It felt impossible that he should be having a DTR talk in front of Maya's parents, who had just found their daughter tangled up with him in the building they were trying to buy, and kept making cryptic comments about it.

"Maya?" Tanner said again.

"What was I supposed to think you meant, Dad!?" Maya yelled. Tanner felt like he couldn't quite get his bearings. What was she talking about? "You handed me a literal blank check and your exact words were 'consider this a blank check in more ways than one'!"

Tanner's chest kept tightening. "Maya?"

Maya looked at him, swallowed hard. She opened her mouth once, then closed it again. Finally, she shook her head. "I'm sorry," she said, then turned and walked to the door. She walked past her parents and into the night without saying a word.

There was a brief moment when everyone left in the room was frozen in place. Then Bruce and Harriett turned and glanced briefly at Tanner before following their daughter into the night.

It was a long time before Tanner could move. Maya's words kept tumbling around in his brain. It sounded to him…it sounded like all of it had been Maya's way of trying to get the old schoolhouse. But it couldn't be…right? She'd even said, hadn't she, earlier in his bed, that she didn't want to talk about the old schoolhouse…?

Tanner had the sudden sensation of walking downstairs and missing a step. He felt disoriented. The Maya he'd come to know and care for wouldn't do something like that.

But maybe he didn't actually know her that well. If he was being honest, it had only been a few weeks, and how well could you really get to know someone in so short a time?

Besides, he thought he was Camille's boyfriend. And it turned out he wasn't.

A lump formed in Tanner's throat. He swallowed hard. He had thought that he and Maya were connected, like she really cared, like he could be something to her. Like they could belong to each other.

But Maya didn't really care about him.

Or, if she did, she cared about the old schoolhouse more. She chose her family over him. She had literally just come over to tell him about the latest way she put her family first.

Suddenly, his love for her loyalty felt like a knife. One of the things he had loved—no, liked—most about her had become a weapon, specifically formulated to make him feel like he was being cut open.

Tanner sat on the couch and buried his head in his hands, trying to catch his breath. None of it was real. The moments with Maya on this couch, in the alleyway, in his bed—all of it was to try to get the old schoolhouse. He felt his hands curling into fists, an urge to hit something coiling in his muscles. He looked around, then his eyes landed on one of the throw pillows on the couch next to him. He turned and drove his fist down into it, over and over again.

When he was spent, he dropped his head between his knees, his chest heaving.

He had to get out of here. Before he hurt something or someone for real. He stood, grabbed his phone and keys and strode out of the old schoolhouse. He didn't make a plan. He just started walking. Down Pine Ridge Avenue. Right on Outpost Way. Up 1st Avenue and up to Tindale Way. He passed the shops that had been familiar to him for years, that had made little homes for themselves in his idiotic heart.

He stopped and turned before he got to the empty storefront where he and Maya had kissed—where she had talked about wanting to open a soap shop.

That had felt so real.

What the fuck am I going to do? He thought. He couldn't imagine staying in town, where every single thing reminded him of Maya. He couldn't fathom serving coffee to the people they both knew, seeing her across the street at the hotel, running into her at the bar or the hardware store or any of the restaurants in town.

But he couldn't leave either. All of his money had been poured into this project of building Sullivan's Coffee. He had no one to go back home to in California—Camille had ended things and Billy was in prison. But more importantly, he didn't want to let go of this dream. It was so important to him, and had been for so long. This coffee shop, in this place, for these people. For his mother. For Billy. For himself.

And he had started to see Maya as part of all of it, too.

The way they could somehow belong to this place together. Belong to each other. He could see that.

God, it hurt.

Tanner lifted one hand and placed it on his chest, where an ache was still pulsing behind his sternum. He felt like he was walking around with part of his heart missing. It occurred to him, almost in passing, that this is probably what it should have felt like when Camille broke up with him.

Tanner stopped in his tracks.

He had been in love with Camille, hadn't he? He was pretty sure. But if this thing with Maya felt this much worse, then that could only mean that…

He was in love with Maya Clark.

The truth of it sliced through him, and the ache in his chest seemed to wrap around his spine and squeeze. He almost couldn't catch his breath for a moment.

The realization couldn't have hit him at a worse time. How could he have been so stupid? To fall for it?

Tanner thought of Maya, her brown hair, her piercing eyes. The ways she made him laugh, the ways she surprised him. How loyal she was to the people close to her. He thought back to her lips pressed against his, the heat of her body in his arms. He clenched his jaw. But, he reminded himself, the Maya he'd fallen in love with wasn't even real. It had all been fake. He didn't need to be broken-hearted over something that wasn't real.

He wasn't mourning anything that could have actually happened. He was grieving a daydream, a castle in the clouds.

He could get over that much quicker.

Okay, so he'd just take the next few weeks and keep his head down. Work his ass off on turning the old school-house into Sullivan's Coffee. Get groceries in Silver Falls.

Maybe text Cosimo if he needed to get out, but they could avoid going anywhere in town. He thought of the poetry night at Pages and Pasta, sitting with Cosimo and Debbie and Maya, Anne and Roberto passing little Tommy between them. His breath caught. He couldn't imagine surviving that if he did it now, being near Maya after everything that had happened between them. But he wouldn't take it away from Maya—all of them were hers first.

So he'd take it away from himself. Until he could survive it again.

Tanner thought back to the way he'd pummeled the pillow at the old schoolhouse and felt a wave of shame wash over him. It was just another reason he and Maya couldn't work anyway, even if she had meant any of it. Because he was fucking volatile. Because no matter what he did, he still had all this violence coiled and waiting inside of him. He refused to become Len. Refused to let the people he cared most about get hurt by being too close to him. Tanner's jaw tightened with resolve, and he swallowed hard.

He knew how to work through bad times. He had done it when his mom died, and when Billy had gone to prison, and throughout his entire childhood and teenage years. He could tune out what he needed to tune out and keep his nose to the grindstone until he could stand to lift his head again.

He pulled out his phone and scrolled to Maya's number. His thumb hovered over the "delete" button for one moment, and then he pressed it. He deleted their few messages, and stuffed his phone back in his pocket. He started walking towards home, trying to focus on his breathing, and not the gaping hole in his chest.

CHAPTER 25

Check Your Oracles

MAYA

Maya walked blindly out of the old schoolhouse.

"Maya, honey!" Harriett's voice called after her.

"I can't talk right now," Maya replied. She got home, strode purposefully up the stairs, into her room, and slammed the door. She began pacing.

The way Tanner had looked at her when he heard what her parents said. About the blank check, about taking the hint. She had wanted to tell him, had tried to explain, but she had frozen. She'd blown up at her parents instead of telling the man she'd come to love how she really felt.

No. Not love. Care about.

Right?

Maya pulled out her phone and dialed Anne's number.

"Hello?"

"I fucked up," Maya said. She heard her voice catch.

"What's going on?"

"My parents caught Tanner and I in the old school-house, and then they said all this shit about the blank check and now Tanner thinks that—"

"Wait, slow down. 'Caught' you and Tanner? Doing what?"

"WHAT DO YOU THINK?" Maya yelled, then added "SORRY FOR YELLING!"

"Okay, let me just…process that part for a second." Anne was quiet while Maya tried to steady her breathing.

"So you and Tanner were…" Anne finally asked.

"Yes."

"And what did your parents say?"

Maya closed her eyes. "Mom was all giddy. She said something about me taking the hint really far, and then Dad said something about how I didn't need to go so far as to make him my boyfriend. And now Tanner probably thinks I was just seducing him for the old schoolhouse."

"Were you?"

Maya felt like the wind was knocked out of her. "How can you ask me that?"

"I'm just trying to understand!" Anne said.

"No, Anne. I was not seducing Tanner to get the old schoolhouse. I know we were joking about this, but I'm not actually going to weaponize sex to get something from someone. I already got slut-shamed by my parents, I don't need it from you."

The line was quiet. When Anne finally spoke, it was in a voice filled with regret. "I'm sorry, Maya. I didn't mean to…I didn't mean it. I should have known better. That was shitty of me."

"Thank you," Maya said.

"So…you and Tanner are…were…? Because you actually like him?"

Maya sat down on her bed. "I think I do. I think he's… I really…he's so good. Yes, he's very attractive, and he's a really good kisser and he's good in bed, but it's…more than that. He's patient and caring and even though he's kind of quiet at first, he just loves so hard, with this enormous heart. And he isn't afraid to laugh at my jokes—he's not all intimidated or stupid about it. And he works so hard, and all of it is because he wants everyone to have what they need."

There was a long pause. "Maya?" Anne asked.

"What?"

"Are you in love with Tanner Sullivan?"

The question hit Maya squarely in the middle of her chest, ramming into her sternum and leaving her a little out of breath.

"I DON'T KNOW!!! MAYBE?!" Maya yelled, throwing one arm up into the air. "You tell me!"

Maya could hear Anne's smile when she spoke next.

"I can't tell you. You've never needed anyone else's guidance to know what you already know. You've got your oracles. Ask them."

A knock came on Maya's door. Maya closed her eyes and took a deep breath. "Do you think it would be possible," Maya asked quietly, "for me to crash with Debbie for a minute? Sleep in your old room?"

"You can stay here if you want," Anne said.

"I know," Maya replied. "I just need…" She thought of Roberto and Anne being in love, the little moments of laughter and affection that made up their days, the way they passed baby Tommy between them, and she wasn't sure if she could stand it.

"Or you can stay with Debbie," Anne added. "I'll text her."

"Thank you," Maya said. Another knock. "Just a minute!" she yelled toward the door.

"Can I call you again later if I need to?" Maya asked, grabbing an overnight bag.

"Of course," Anne said. "Love you."

"Love you, too."

Maya hung up, then paused and walked towards her door. She took a deep breath. "I can't talk right now," she said through the door. "I'm staying with Debbie for a few nights. Please find someone to cover my shifts at the hotel. I'll talk to you after that." Maya waited, then heard slow footsteps making their way towards her parents' room. She listened for the quiet snick of the door clicking closed.

Guilt flooded her stomach. But for once in her life, she was going to take the time to figure her shit out.

HALF AN HOUR LATER, Maya was sitting cross-legged on Anne's old bed, Debbie having let her in and given her a cup of tea, telling her to stay as long as she needed. Maya pulled out her deck of tarot cards and shuffled them. Anne had told her to ask her oracles, so that's what she was doing. She couldn't bring herself to ask the point-blank question "Am I in love with Tanner Sullivan?" So instead she just whispered, "Give me guidance" and knocked on the cards before pulling three from the deck.

The Fool. Maya hung her head. "Fine, call me out," she said. She already knew she'd been an idiot—she didn't need an oracle to tell her that. But Maya forced herself to think beyond her own self-loathing for a moment. The Fool was about more than just idiocy. It was a card of new beginnings, where the need to change is greater than the fear of change. Yes, the fool was inexperienced, but that wasn't stopping him. *Or her, as the case may be,* Maya thought. She turned over the next card.

The King of Wands. A card of action. A character of fierce optimism, of so much confidence that it doesn't occur to him that he might fail. He just goes for things without worrying about them.

Which was not how Maya felt at the moment. This particular tarot reading was feeling mean. She'd asked for guidance, not being read to filth. She flipped over the last card.

The Tower.

"Ugh, what do you want from me?!" Maya said to the card.

Then she paused.

Her words echoed in her head.

What do you want?

She thought back to Tanner, asking her that question in the alleyway, in the bar, in his bed.

What did Maya actually want?

When he'd asked her that under the tree, all those weeks ago, she'd spoken without thinking. The soap shop. Maya pulled out her journal and opened to the page where she'd started a "want list."

I want Tanner Sullivan to make me come with his tongue.

I want Tanner Sullivan to fuck me.

I want

Well, she could mark the first two items off the list. Check, complete. Maya smiled in spite of herself, memories of Tanner's hands gripping the back of her thighs, his mouth hot on her skin. She closed her eyes.

She wanted more of that. She pulled out a pen and wrote "I want more of Tanner Sullivan." She took a breath, and with shaking hands, added, "I want to open a soap shop."

Maya thought back to conversations with Tanner, after her parents had given her and Devan the hotel. She opened to a new page and wrote "I Don't Want." Underneath that, she wrote "I don't want to own or run the hotel." And then, with a breath of clarity, she wrote, "I actually don't want to work at the hotel at all."

She sat back and looked at the words she'd written so far. It wasn't much, but it was a start. She closed her eyes. *What do you want?*

Maya tried to imagine her ideal life. Her breath caught as images began to form in her mind. A small soap shop here in West Tindale. Scarves and tarot cards and candles in the window. Tanner bringing her coffee from Sullivan's, kissing her while she stood behind the register. Her heart beat faster in her chest.

Are you in love with Tanner Sullivan?

Anne's question echoed in Maya's mind. If she was honest, she wasn't sure if she'd ever actually been in love. She wasn't sure she knew what it felt like. She'd been insanely attracted to people, cared deeply about them, enjoyed being around them. But she'd never felt about anyone the way she felt about Tanner. Like…he made everything clearer. Like he was a port in a storm. Like being near him uncoiled everything in her spine and made it hum with rightness.

"Fuck," Maya whispered. "I'm in love with Tanner Sullivan."

Maya's phone rang. For one glorious, adrenaline-filled moment, she hoped it was Tanner. But the name on the screen was Devan.

Maya answered. "Hey," she said.

"Hey," Devan replied. The two of them sat in silence for a moment.

"Are you in Silver Falls?" Maya asked.

"Yeah," Devan said. He paused, then added, "You can come hang out here if you need."

Maya smiled sadly. "I'm at Debbie's, in Anne's old room. Things got…worse after you left." Maya stumbled through an explanation about their parents finding her and Tanner in the old schoolhouse, how their parents reacted, and what she'd said and done. She fought tears the entire time.

"So does Tanner…what does Tanner think?" Devan asked.

"I don't know," Maya said. "I haven't talked to him yet."

"What are you going to say when you do?"

Maya thought. "I feel like I need a…plan. Maybe it's because I'm staying in Anne's old room right now, and she's all about plans, but I think everything is fucked up enough for me to need a plan." She was quiet for a moment. "And not just with Tanner Sullivan," she added. "It feels like…like something has shifted in our family. Kind of…permanently." The two siblings sat in silence for a moment. "Do you know how long you're staying in Silver Falls?" Maya asked.

Devan sighed. "Probably a week at least. I know that sucks, but I just can't come home."

"I'm proud of you, you know," Maya said quietly. "For standing up to them."

"It was a long time coming," Devan replied. After a pause, he added, "What are you going to do?"

"About which part?"

"Our parents. The hotel."

Maya laid back on the bed and stared at the ceiling. "I don't know yet," she said. "But whatever *you* do, I'm on your team. Whether you decide to come back and work but not take over, or take over, or stay in Silver Falls forever, or whatever. I support you."

"Thanks," Devan said. "Do you want any help coming up with your plan?"

Maya sat up and glanced down at the tarot cards still

spread out on the bedspread. "I think I need to figure this one out on my own," Maya said. "Without worrying about what anyone else thinks. But I'll call you if I change my mind."

"Good. Hey, I love you," Devan said.

Maya smiled, her heart warming. "I love you, too," she replied. "We don't say that often enough."

"Maybe we can start."

"I'll plan on it."

After they hung up, Maya turned to a new page in her journal. And began writing.

CHAPTER 26

You Can't Help Your Feelings

TANNER

Tanner managed to avoid going anywhere but his apartment and the old schoolhouse for four full days. He worked at a manic pace—replacing baseboards and ordering tables and fixing the plumbing. He usually had music playing while he worked, which helped keep his thoughts from becoming too loud. Most nights he stayed at the old schoolhouse until 9 or 10 pm, then went home exhausted. He showered and fell right into bed.

That first night had been awful. Memories of Maya filled every corner of his bedroom, but he didn't have anywhere else to sleep. He needed to find a couch, and soon. But was he just going to sleep on the couch for the rest of his life? He refused to let Maya's ghost keep him from sleeping in his enormous carved wooden bed. He'd folded his arms and jammed his eyes shut until he finally fell asleep.

He hadn't talked to anyone. While he and Cosimo had become friends, they weren't quite good enough friends for Tanner to unburden himself about all of this. Plus, Cosimo was Roberto's brother, and Roberto was married to Anne, who was Maya's best friend, and it felt like the loyalties there were a little stacked against him.

Figuring out how to live in West Tindale, when every part of it was connected to Maya, was tearing him up inside. This is what he had meant when he talked about being afraid of the wanting. This is what he had been afraid of. The gutting, tragic, horrible loss of it all. The way it was so hopeful at first, so goddamn beautiful…the way he felt he could belong somewhere, for the first time in his life. Now it felt like his heart had been literally carved out of his chest.

He'd survived worse things, he knew. Objectively speaking, having your dad beat the shit out of you and your family was way more traumatic than a girl you liked not being into you.

It just seemed to hurt a lot worse in the moment.

But as he stood in the old schoolhouse at 8 pm, staring at the wall and thinking about Maya, he decided to use a lifeline. He pulled out his phone and called California State Prison Solano. It took him a while to navigate the automated system, but eventually he was able to leave a message for Billy.

"Hey, man. I'm just…I'm going through some shit and thought it would be good to talk. Call me when you can."

Tanner had gotten halfway through re-sealing one of the windows when his phone rang. He answered to a robotic voice. "You have a call from an inmate at a California State Correctional Facility. To accept the call, press 1."

Tanner pressed 1 and waited. Billy's voice came through.

"Hey," he said.

Tanner was flooded with relief to hear his brother's voice. "Hey," he replied.

"Oh shit, she dumped you," Billy said.

Tanner was astounded, and frankly, a little insulted. "How did…? She didn't dump me."

"Well, something happened," Billy said. "You sound sad as hell."

Tanner sighed and sat down. "Turns out she was faking it."

"Faking *it?*"

Thoughts of Maya in his bed came flooding into his mind, the way her legs clenched around him in the heat of it. His stomach sank. "Oh shit," Tanner said. "I hadn't even thought of that."

"What the hell were *you* talking about, then?"

"All of it," Tanner said. "She was trying to get the old schoolhouse. Her family wanted to buy it and she… seduced me."

Billy whistled low. "Shit," he said.

"Yeah. Shit."

There was a long pause. Finally, Billy spoke. "Are you sure, man? Like, how did you find out?"

Tanner told him about Maya's parents walking in on them in the old schoolhouse, about what they'd said, how Maya had reacted.

"And you haven't talked to her since?" Billy asked.

"No," Tanner replied. "But even if I could…"

"Is she not worth it to you?"

"If it was real, it would be. She would be."

"Be honest, dude," Billy said.

"I think…" Tanner placed a hand on his heart. "I think I love her? Like, I'm…in love with her? Or…in love with who I thought she was."

"Okay."

"If it was real, then I'm in love with her."

"But…?"

A wave of shame washed over Tanner.

"It's not just that it was probably fake," he said. "It's… after she left that night, I…I lost it, man. I beat the shit out of a throw pillow. I can't…I hate feeling that way. I don't want anyone to get hurt."

"You don't want to be Len."

Tanner nodded, swallowing hard, before remembering that his brother couldn't see him. "Right," he said.

"Did you hit *her*?" Billy asked.

Tanner blinked. "What the fuck, Billy? No, I didn't hit her."

"You just beat the hell out of a throw pillow?"

"Yeah."

"So like, what therapists always told me to do."

"That's not—"

"You took your feelings and you did something with them that helped you and didn't hurt anyone."

"That's not the point," Tanner said, his voice rising slightly. "I shouldn't have felt that way at all."

"You can't help what you feel," Billy replied. "You can just choose what to do with the feelings."

Tanner frowned and shook his head. "You don't get it."

"Listen to me, man. You're my older brother, but you're being stupid right now. I absolutely fucking get it. And I'm telling you, you're not Len. Len wouldn't have given a shit about hitting a pillow. That's the difference between him and you. He never thought about other people. And that's literally all you do. You're always making sure everyone's safe. Making sure everyone's comfortable. You care so goddamn much, you got mad at yourself for doing something that didn't even hurt anyone."

Tanner stood, breathing hard. He didn't know what to say.

"I know I just laid a bunch of shit on you, man," Billy said. "But I'm gonna do it some more. Real quick. Just one more thing."

"What is it?" Tanner said, resigned.

"I think you should talk to her," Billy said. "Just check in. It sounds like emotions were running high and you don't want to jump to any conclusions."

Tanner smiled, despite the riot of emotion he was feeling. "How did you get so fucking wise?"

"Hours of state-mandated therapy, dude."

"They should mandate it for everyone."

The two brothers sat in silence for a moment. Finally Tanner spoke.

"Thanks, Billy," he said. "I mean it."

"Anytime, big brother."

After he hung up, Tanner stared at the wall for a long time. Was it possible that he had misinterpreted what had happened that night with Maya? When her parents found them? He tried to replay the things she had said—her actual words, and not just what he assumed they meant. And if he was being really honest, he found that they were actually kind of…ambiguous?

But then why hadn't she reached out? Why hadn't she come to see him at the old schoolhouse while he was working, or texted, or called?

Well, why hadn't *he*?

Maybe they were both just stupidly waiting for the other one to say something. He glanced at his phone. He'd text, but he'd deleted Maya's number, like an idiot. He looked out the window over at the hotel.

Tomorrow. He'd find her and talk to her tomorrow.

He stood up and began pacing. What would he say?

First of all, he needed to know if it was real. If the things they said and did together meant something. He needed to know if he was a pawn in some grand plan of seduction to get the old schoolhouse. Because if he was, then the rest wouldn't matter. But if he wasn't…

If he wasn't, what did he want? He spent so long asking Maya that question that he hadn't really stopped to ask himself in a while.

He wanted Maya. Of course he wanted Maya. But he wanted her to choose him—all of him. He wanted to be her boyfriend, and to have her be his girlfriend. Nothing casual, nothing "low-commitment."

Tanner knew that if Maya wanted something low commitment, it was going to be the most difficult thing in the world to say no. Because he wanted her, and it was tempting to just take anything she could offer him. But he deserved more than just the crumbs of someone's affection. He didn't want another Camille situation.

God, he hoped Maya would say yes. Well, that she would say no to the first question ("was it fake?") and yes to the second question ("will you be my girlfriend?").

He felt like he was in middle school. Or how he imagined he would have felt in middle school if he'd ever had the courage to pass a girl a note with the classic "Do you like me? Circle yes or no."

The thought of basically having a real-time conversation version of that with Maya tomorrow made him feel like he was being forced to jump out of an airplane.

But he knew what he wanted. If anyone was worth jumping for, it was Maya.

CHAPTER 27

Saying What Needs to be Said

MAYA

At 9 pm two days after moving in to Anne's old room, Maya took a deep breath and walked up the stairs to her family's apartment in the hotel. She walked to her parents' door, her journal under her arm, and knocked.

Bruce opened the door and surprise flashed across his face. Maya could see past him into the room, where Harriett was sitting in bed with her laptop. When she saw Maya, her lips drew into a thin line, and she folded her arms and turned away. Maya's heart sank, but she took a deep breath and spoke anyway.

"Hey Mom and Dad," Maya said. "Can I talk to you?"

Bruce glanced at Harriett, then opened the door wide. "Your mother might not be ready to talk, but we'll listen to what you have to say."

Maya took another steadying breath and stepped into the room. Bruce sat down beside his wife, and Maya took a seat on the edge of the bed.

"I've been doing a lot of thinking," she started, "And I—"

"What took you so long to talk to us?" Harriett interrupted. Her eyes were filled with tears.

Maya closed her eyes for a moment. "I can explain everything, but I need you to just listen for a minute."

Bruce put his hand over his wife's, then turned to Maya and nodded. "We're listening."

"Thank you. I'm sorry I haven't talked to you before now. I needed some time and space to figure some things out." Maya opened her journal. "Have you ever heard of a 'want list'?" she asked.

"Like a wish list?" Harriet replied.

Maya smiled and nodded. "Like a wish list. I've realized over the past few weeks that I'm not very good at saying what I want. But someone really…dear to me explained how…powerful, or…meaningful it can be. To claim what you want." Maya's heart sped up, thinking of Tanner, the way he would look at her whenever he asked her what she wanted. "For a long time, I knew deep down what I wanted, and what I didn't want, but I wasn't brave enough to claim it. But I'm trying to do that now."

"Well, tell us," Harriet said.

Maya felt her throat getting tight, and tears pricked behind her eyes, but she knew she had to do this. She looked down at her journal and read out loud.

"I don't want to run the hotel. I want to expand my soap business and open a shop here in town. And I don't want to live with my parents forever."

When she looked back up, it was to see tears in both Bruce and Harriet's eyes. It was killing her, seeing them upset like this, knowing she was the cause of it. The feeling was crushing for a moment. One part of her wanted to just close her journal, forget the whole thing, tell her parents she didn't mean it. But she knew she had to do this. She looked back down.

"I also know how important family is to you," she said, "And I want to tell you how grateful I am for everything you've done for me and Devan." And she meant it. Even if she didn't want the exact things her parents offered her, it was meaningful to know that they were offering something. She knew not everyone had the privilege of attentive parents. She took another deep breath.

"But if I'm going to live my life the way I truly want to, I need some independence."

Her words hung in the room for a few moments, Maya still looking down at her journal in her lap. Harriett was the first to talk.

"What does that even look like? Independence? Don't we give you independence?"

Maya chose to ignore the last question and focused on the first one.

"I'm going to stay with Debbie in Anne's old room for a few months," she said. "And then eventually, get my own apartment."

"What about the hotel?"

Maya looked up. Her parents looked weary. "I'll help you find and hire additional staff," she said. "I'm willing to work another three months to help cover things while you find someone to replace me."

"And Devan?" Bruce asked.

"That's between you and Devan."

There was a long pause as Maya gathered her thoughts and breath for the last thing she needed to say. "And I won't be helping you to get the old schoolhouse. I won't tell you what to do, but I think you should let Tanner" (her voice caught on his name) "keep it. It's important to him."

Maya stood up. She'd gotten through it. "I know…I know this is hard. But thank you for listening. I love you both." Maya paused, then walked around to her mom's side of the bed and put her arms around her. Harriett didn't hug her back right away, but then her arms came around her for a quick pat. Maya circled to the other side of the bed and hugged Bruce, who held her tightly for one tiny moment, and then broke the hug off.

Then Maya left the room and tried to stop herself from bursting into tears. She'd save that for when she got back to Anne's old place.

IT HAD BEEN years since Maya fully sobbed the way she just had for the last half hour. She had definitely cried after her parents found her at the old schoolhouse with Tanner—after they had said what they did and Tanner had looked at her and she had frozen, not knowing what to say. She'd wanted to text him, call him, reach out, but she was just… too humiliated. But more than that, he probably hated her. He probably didn't want anything to do with her. She'd walked out on him. Like so many other people in his life. So she'd taken the high road and saved him from herself, and was using this time to figure her shit out.

When she finally lifted her head from the pillow in Anne's old room, she felt exhausted, but clear-headed. Her face was puffy and red, her nose was runny, and tissues surrounded her. She was sure her hair was also a mess. But she knew she had done the right thing. Or at least the thing she needed to do. The thing that, deep down, she wanted to do.

A soft knock came on the door. Maya wiped her nose and said "Come in."

Debbie and Anne stepped in, and Maya almost burst into a fresh wave of tears. Anne held a bottle of wine and Debbie held a plate of lasagna.

"I think I manifested this without even knowing it," Maya said.

"Lucky for you we're magic, too," Debbie said, stepping inside and sitting on the bed, handing the plate and a fork to Maya.

"We picked up on your manifesting and answered the call," Anne added, unscrewing the bottle of wine and handing it over. "Also, we didn't bring glasses but who cares, we're all basically family anyway."

"There's still time for you to marry Cosimo!" Debbie said, elbowing Maya.

"Mom, I don't understand why you can never remember that Cosimo is gay," Anne said.

"It can be a marriage of convenience! Tax purposes, family reunions," Debbie replied.

Maya laughed. "I will happily marry Cosimo if I get to come to your family reunions."

"You get to come anyway," Anne said. "You're Tommy's godmother. Speaking of family…how did it go?"

Maya sighed. "It was hard as hell and I cried and they cried, but I said what I needed to say."

Debbie put her arm around Maya. "I'm proud of you, hon," she said.

"You're a rock star," Anne added.

"I feel like a…soggy rock star," Maya replied, taking a sip of the wine.

This earned another squeeze around the shoulders from Debbie, and Anne laid her hand over Maya's. "Even the best of rock stars get soggy sometimes," Anne said.

Maya felt a lump rise in her throat, and she was afraid she was going to cry again, this time from gratitude. "You should cross-stitch that on a pillow."

"So," Debbie said. "Now what?"

Maya heaved an enormous sigh. "Now I come up with

a business plan for the Tindale Soap Company. I talk to Ruby at the real estate office. Then fundraising, graphic design, all of the things. Anne, wanna help with some of the design stuff?"

"Please let me help with design stuff!" Anne said. "I want to think about something other than diapers and bottles and sleep and teeth."

Maya smiled and squeezed her hand.

"And Tanner?" Debbie asked quietly.

A fist tightened around Maya's chest, an ache that she'd been trying to ignore now making itself felt. Maya shrugged forlornly.

"Last time we talked," Anne said slowly, "You said you might be in love with Tanner Sullivan. Have you…investigated that any further?"

Maya nodded.

"And?"

Maya nodded again.

"But it doesn't matter," she added. "I was so shitty to him—I just froze and walked out on him and he hasn't called or texted or anything, so I don't think he's…that there's anything…there."

The three women sat in silence for a moment. "Has it occurred to you," Debbie said, "That he might be waiting on you?"

Maya swallowed. It hadn't occurred to her. Which seemed…really stupid, now that she thought about it. She was the one who'd left him in the lurch, without explanation. It made sense that she should be the one to reach out first.

"What do I do?" Maya said.

"I don't think you need some grand gesture," Anne replied. "You can just…Notting Hill it. You know, 'I'm just a girl standing in front of a boy'…"

"I don't know what to say," Maya said.

"I just told you what to say," Anne replied. "'I'm just a girl standing in front of a boy…'"

Debbie stood and pulled a chair up to the edge of the bed. "Practice on us," she said. "What do you want to say?"

So Maya did. For the next hour, she tried to find the right words, working with these strong, compassionate women who'd loved her for her entire life. By the time she finally went to sleep, she had a plan for tomorrow.

CHAPTER 28

Halfway Across the Street

TANNER

T anner was terrified. He'd spent twenty minutes trying to pick a shirt that morning, before finally putting on a green button-up that Camille once said brought out his eyes. Then he paced his living room for another twenty minutes.

Finally, he stood still and took a deep breath. "Fuck it," he said. He grabbed his keys and started walking towards the old schoolhouse.

He had decided to wait until the workday was over to talk to Maya. He didn't want to interrupt her day, and if she was about to reject him, he didn't want to spend the rest of the day trying to work when he felt like shit. (And he knew he'd feel like shit.)

Tanner laid his green button-up on the couch in the old schoolhouse and spent the morning rearranging the furniture, trying to find the right layout, but he could barely concentrate. Thoughts of Maya, of what he planned to say, kept racing through his brain. He kept measuring furniture and then forgetting their measurements, putting things down and then forgetting where he put them. By noon, he had made almost no progress on the furniture layout and he was ready to tear his hair out.

His phone dinged with a text. For a moment, he hoped against hope that it was Maya. But Cosimo's name came up.

> Hey you want lunch?

Tanner sighed. He did want lunch. And he did not want to try and figure out where to go or what to do for lunch. Too much of his brain was occupied by thoughts of Maya. He fired off a quick "sure thanks" and put his phone in his back pocket.

He threw his shirt on and kept his head down as he passed the Hitchin' Post Hotel. He didn't look up until he was ready to cross Pine Ridge Avenue to get to Pages and Pasta. The few cars that were on the street moved slowly, the lazy speed of tourists in a small town. Then Tanner looked up and saw Maya. She standing on the other side of the street, looking both ways.

Tanner's breath caught. He'd somehow forgotten how beautiful she was. A few strands of hair in waves framed her face, tendrils being lifted by the breeze. She wore a summery dress, something covered in strawberries, half of her hair caught up in a colorful scarf. He reached up and placed a hand over his heart.

Just then, Maya looked across the street and her eyes met his. And she looked…she looked caring. Nervous. Tender.

Loving.

Long moments passed between them. Then she yelled his name.

"Tanner!"

Tanner didn't realize he was running until it was happening. "Maya!" he yelled back.

And then she was running towards him, and flying into his arms, and he was lifting her off her feet, there in the middle of the road. It felt so good to hold her. His whole body was filled with the rightness of it. There were still things to be said, but for this moment, he needed to just feel her there against him. He spun them slowly around once, twice, before setting her gently on her feet. He took her face in his hands.

"Maya," he said.

Maya rested both of her hands on his chest. "I missed you," she said.

Tanner's heart stuttered, then leaped. "Do you mean that?" he said quietly.

"Of course I do," Maya said, frowning slightly.

Tanner took a deep breath. "I wasn't sure if…"

Maya reached up and stroked his face. "I am so sorry," she said. "I'm sorry for walking out that day, and for not calling or texting you. I needed a minute to figure some things out."

Tanner's next breath was a little shaky. "And what did you figure out?"

Maya smiled. "A whole bunch of things. But I know that I want you."

Fireworks exploded in Tanner's chest. But he wanted to be sure. He paused, then asked, "Like, in a sex way or a friend way or a boyfriend way?"

Maya's smile widened. "I mean, honestly, all of the above."

The fireworks in Tanner's chest were now being accompanied by a symphony. A brass band. A cheer squad. His head was so full of celebration, he could barely think. It was taking him a minute to process any of this. He still had so many things he needed to ask, so many things he needed to understand and make sure of, but Maya was looking up at him with so much sincerity that the walls he had put up were quickly crumbling.

"You want to be my girlfriend?" Tanner asked.

Maya answered by reaching up to grab his collar and pulling his face down to hers. When she kissed him, it was with so much certainty, so much joy, that Tanner wrapped his arms around Maya and lifted her off her feet again. He kissed her lips fiercely, then set her down and kissed her nose, her cheeks, her eyelids, her forehead—any part of her he could reach. He felt her quiet laughter and he grinned in response, his lips still resting on her forehead.

"You want to be my girlfriend?" he repeated, this time in a whisper.

"I want to be your girlfriend," Maya whispered back, her voice low and full of promise. He could hear the smile in her voice when she said it. Heat flooded his body.

"Is that the only thing you want?" Tanner whispered, his lips brushing Maya's ear as he spoke, making her shiver.

"I'll tell you the rest later," she replied, a little breathless. She turned her face and kissed him again, her lips hot and longing against his. Tanner wrapped his hands around Maya's waist and pulled her body flush to him, his mouth hungry for her.

A car horn blared and Maya and Tanner pulled apart.

"We should probably get out of the middle of the street," Tanner said quietly.

"If they can stop for bison, they can stop for us." Maya leaned in to pick up where they'd just left off, but Tanner laughed and took her hand. They ran across the street toward the old schoolhouse.

A voice yelled from across the street. "Hey, did you want lunch or not?"

Tanner turned to see Cosimo standing outside of Pages and Pasta, his hands on his hips, a wide grin on his face.

"Later!" Tanner said.

Once inside the building, Tanner shut the door. He wanted desperately to pull Maya to him, but he just…he had to be sure.

"Maya," he said quietly. "Was it real? Us?" He watched Maya's face. She took a step toward him and his stomach lurched. She put her hands on either side of his face. "Tanner," she said. "Every single thing I did with you was absolutely real. I did it because I wanted to."

Something warm was spreading through Tanner's chest. Because he believed her. All of the relief and joy he had been feeling multiplied inside of him, and he leaned down to plant his lips on hers. She opened her mouth to him and his hands moved over her body. He pushed Maya against the door, and he felt her arching her back to meet him, her hands moving over him with the same desperation he felt. He suddenly felt too impatient to be gentle, and he could feel the same thing in Maya's body, in the hungry way she moved against him.

"Curtains," Maya said, breathless.

"Fuck the curtains," Tanner said, his hands and lips still busy.

Maya laughed. "No, I want you to fuck *me*," she said. She pulled away enough to look him in the face. "So close the curtains."

Tanner practically sprinted around the room, yanking the curtains closed. When he came back, he lifted Maya off her feet, his hands cupping her ass as he walked them quickly to the counter on the other side of the room. He set her down and stood between her legs, lifting her dress over her head.

Maya reached forward and with fumbling hands, she unbuckled his belt and unzipped his pants. Tanner planted both of his hands on the counter on either side of her hips as she pulled his cock out, already hard and aching for her.

She spit in her hand and reached down, wrapping her fingers around him. She was moving quickly, pumping him in her fist with so much lust in her eyes Tanner could hardly stay standing. He clenched his teeth, his breath getting shallower by the second.

"Maya, sweetheart, I…" he gritted out. Then he pulled her roughly from the counter. He knew there was a couch nearby, but he wasn't going to make it that far. He brought both of them down to the floor and when Maya was underneath him, he yanked her panties aside. He hadn't even taken his pants fully off, but there wasn't time for that either.

He had his dick in his hand when he suddenly paused. He could barely think straight, with Maya hot and flushed in front of him, but he managed to whisper roughly, "Condom?"

Maya reached her arms up around his neck and shook her head. "I'm on the pill." Her voice sounded as rough as his. "Please," she said. "I want you inside me."

Tanner didn't wait another second. He positioned himself and then plunged into her. He and Maya's moans echoed in the old schoolhouse as their bodies met.

"You're perfect," he whispered. "God, you're so perfect."

Maya reached down and clutched his hips, urging him to move faster.

It didn't take long. Within minutes, Tanner felt Maya

shudder beneath him, and his own release came seconds later.

Tanner collapsed onto her, this extraordinary woman.

His girlfriend.

He was seeing stars.

"I love you," Maya whispered.

Tanner lifted his head to look at her.

"I know it might be too soon," she said, "But I love you."

Tanner pressed his lips against Maya's cheek. "I love you," he said. He repeated it as he kissed her jaw, her neck, her shoulder, her collarbones. "I love you, I love you, I love you."

CHAPTER 29

The Want List

MAYA

When they had cleaned up and put themselves back together, Maya and Tanner sat on the couch facing each other.

Maya didn't think she had ever seen anyone so handsome in her entire life. His broad shoulders. His curly hair, messy from their lovemaking. His tender hazel eyes. When he smiled gently at her, she thought she might float right off the couch with happiness.

"I made a Want List," Maya said.

Tanner raised his eyebrows. "Yeah?" His smile widened. "What's on it?"

"You, for one thing," Maya replied. "You're actually like, the first *several* things."

"Several things?"

Maya listed the items off on her fingers. "One, I want Tanner Sullivan to make me come with his tongue. Check. Two, I want Tanner Sullivan to fuck me. Check. Three, I want Tanner Sullivan to be my boyfriend. Check."

Tanner looked at Maya with so much affection that it

made her breathe catch. He leaned in to kiss her smile. "What else do you want?"

"I want to move out of my parents' place." Another kiss. "And…" Maya's smile fell just a little, and she took a shuddering breath. "I want to quit the hotel."

She still felt terrified about that part. She knew it was the right thing to do, and what she needed and wanted to do, but decades of family pressures didn't disappear overnight. Tanner pulled away and nodded at her, one hand on the side of her face. "And after that?" he asked.

"After that, I want to open a soap shop in town. And that's it for now."

"That's a pretty good list," Tanner replied, leaning in to kiss her again.

They spent a few more moments kissing, slow and tender. These kisses weren't the hot, desperate kisses of hunger, but the quiet kisses of coming home to each other. After a little while, Tanner asked, "Have you talked to your parents? About quitting?"

Maya nodded. The memory of that talk with Bruce and Harriett still stung. She was still tempted to go back, tell them she had made a mistake, apologize, go back to the way things were. But she knew she couldn't.

"How did it go?" Tanner asked, resting his elbow on the back of the couch, his head leaning on his hand.

"It was okay." Maya paused. "Actually, it was hard as hell, and I'm still not sure if I did it well, but I'm glad I did it. It was time."

"I never know how to say this without it sounding a little condescending, but I'm really proud of you."

To her surprise, tears sprung to Maya's eyes. She looked at the floor, brushing them away quickly.

"Thank you," she said. "It's not condescending. It means a lot."

"I love you," Tanner said.

Maya met his eyes. "I love you, too." She leaned in to kiss him, then sighed. "I told them I would stay on for three more months. I'm going to stay in Anne's old room for a little while, above Pages and Pasta. Then hopefully get my own place."

"Want to move in with me?"

Maya raised her eyebrows. They had just become official less than an hour ago. And while her heart leapt at the thought of sharing Tanner's apartment, she still paused.

"Is that…wise?" she asked.

Tanner shrugged. "You don't have to, but the offer is there whenever you want it."

Maya looked at him. "You seem a little nonchalant about an offer to move in together." Tanner returned her look, his eyes roaming over her face. Maya swallowed. "Like, I appreciate the offer, but I only want to do it if it's what you really want."

"I want you to move in with me," Tanner said. "I want you in my apartment all the time so that I can bend you over every piece of furniture I have."

"That's like, two pieces of furniture," Maya said, a teasing grin on her face.

"I'll get more," Tanner replied. "I'll buy furniture with the express purpose of fucking you on it." He reached out and took a lock of her hair, twisting it gently in his fingers.

"While I love the sound of that," Maya said, "I don't have to be living there for it to happen."

Tanner took a deep breath. "I know. And I don't want to pressure you. I'm just…sure. About you. About us."

Maya looked at him. She reached up and ran her hand through his hair. Now that she *could* touch him all the time, she didn't ever want to stop. His eyes fell closed at the brush of her fingers.

"Let me think about it," Maya said. "Not because I'm not sure about you, but because I want to know I'm moving out of my parents' place because I want to, and not because I just want you."

Tanner opened his eyes and studied her for a moment, and then he nodded. "I understand that."

"You're not…is that okay?"

Tanner smiled. "Yes, that's okay. If it's ever not, I'll tell you."

Maya flopped backward on the couch. "Why is he so perfect?!" she asked the ceiling.

Tanner's form took up her line of vision, as he hovered over her. "I'm just reflecting what you are," he said.

"Come here and kiss me," Maya said, reaching her arms around his neck.

Tanner obliged, and as his lips met hers, Maya had the sensation of her whole life falling into place. She was right where she belonged.

Sometime later, after they came up for air, Tanner pulled Maya into his arms and settled her head on his chest.

"Can I ask you something?" he asked.

Maya nodded.

Tanner seemed to deliberate for a few moments. He seemed suddenly nervous, and Maya felt her stomach drop. She raised her head to look up at him, and his eyes were filled with anxiety.

"What is it?" she asked, her brow furrowed in concern.

"Did your parents…did they suggest…that you uh, seduce me? To get the old schoolhouse?"

Maya squeezed her eyes shut. A wave of shame washed over her. "They—" she started. She took a deep breath. "They did say 'consider this a blank check in more ways than one' when they gave me the money." Maya re-opened her eyes to look at Tanner. "But that's not what I did. That's not what I was doing. I wanted you anyway. I still want you."

Tanner looked into her face, then nodded. "Thank you," he said. "I was pretty sure, I just…that day when your parents walked in on us—"

Maya groaned and fell back into Tanner's chest. "Ugh, don't remind me."

"Aside from being just…embarrassing, it was also… confusing. I couldn't figure out what anyone was talking about, and when you left, I just started making assumptions."

Maya ached for him. For the days he must have spent thinking she didn't care for him.

"I'm sorry about that," Tanner said.

Maya pulled away and looked up at him. "*You're* sorry?! What the fuck are *you* sorry for?"

"For making assumptions," Tanner said. "For following my own terrified thoughts to the worst conclusion, instead of talking to you first."

"*I'm* sorry I didn't talk to *you*. I'm sorry you even had the opportunity to think I didn't care about you."

"I did get a lot done on this place during those days," Tanner said.

Maya sat up even further. "I have one more thing on my Want List," she said. "I want you to have the old schoolhouse." Tanner raised his eyebrows at her and she paused. "I know it's already yours, but I'm going to stop trying to get you to give it to my parents. If I'm being completely honest, I don't think I ever actually wanted you to give it up. Or if I did, I stopped pretty quickly. Because I know it's important to you. And it's really beautiful. What you've done. What you're doing. The way you're building this place of comfort and safety and goodness."

To Maya's surprise, Tanner's eyes filled with tears.

"Oh, honey!" she said, reaching forward to hold his face.

He leaned forward until his forehead was resting against hers. "Thank you," he said quietly. "I'm so fucking scared of turning into my father sometimes. But I'm trying to trust that I'm…the fact that you see what I'm trying to do and that you love those things…that means the world to me." He pressed his lips gently to Maya's for a brief moment.

"Anyone who knows anything about you can see that you care so deeply for other people," Maya said. "It's one of the reasons I fell in love with you."

This time Tanner leaned back and asked the ceiling, "Why is she so perfect!?"

Maya didn't think she could grin any wider.

"Come here," she said.

"Why? What do you want?" Tanner asked, turning to her and smiling.

Maya took his face in her hands and planted a kiss on his lips. "You," she whispered.

Maya climbed up onto a crate and waved to the crowd gathered on the sidewalk of Tindale Way. "Thank you all for coming to the grand opening of West Tindale's newest soap and candle shop, The Wick and Bubble!" A cheer arose, and Maya caught Tanner grinning at her from the sidewalk. "I'm so excited to open the doors to all of you, my friends and family, and I couldn't have done it without your support." Maya glanced out over the crowd, and for a moment, she felt a lump build in her throat. Debbie and Cosimo were there, and Anne and Roberto with a squirming Tommy perched on his shoulders. (How was he already a *toddler*?!) There was Kenny and the Zhaos and the handful of friends she'd known since high school who were still here with families of their own. Devan had come up from Silver Falls for the occasion, and there, toward the back, stood her parents.

Maya swallowed and smiled out at the crowd again. "Everything is half-off today, so be sure to grab your favorites. But if you don't grab them now, we'll be open all summer, and Wick and Bubble products will be available at

Sullivan's Coffee, the West Tindale Visitor's Center, various small shops around town, and at Club Wyndham, formerly known as The Hitchin' Post Hotel." Another round of applause. "And now, I'll get off my *soap box*," Maya said with a wink, to a few groans and polite laughs, "And let you check out West Tindale's newest tourist trap!"

The small crowd gave a final cheer, and Maya stepped down from her crate and opened the door to her new little shop.

She still couldn't quite believe it was real. Real and *hers*. She and Tanner had spent the winter painting and cleaning the little space she had first seen last spring. Anne had helped her brainstorm a name for her shop, and Maya liked that "The Wick and Bubble" had vaguely witchy connotations while still describing what she sold. Maya had also come up with fifteen new scents and their accompanying names were as punny as she could make them.

Maya stood behind the register while customers wandered in the tiny space, which was honestly way too small for an event like this, but Maya was too happy to care. Tanner made his way through the crowd and stepped behind the register, leaning down to plant a kiss on her forehead. "How's it going?" he said quietly.

"Better than I even imagined," Maya grinned up at him.

Tanner returned her smile, and her heart leaped a little at the way it made his hazel eyes light up, crinkles at their corners. "Do you need anything?"

"Do you have time to get my phone charger from our place?" she said. "I think it's under the couch?"

Tanner frowned. "Why would it be *under* the couch?"

"Well, it was *on* the couch, but then last night happened on the couch, and it—"

Tanner held up his hand and smiled. "Got it. I can go

grab it. And I wanted to check and see if the new coffee table got delivered."

"Good call," Maya said. "We're running out of furniture for you to bend me over."

Tanner's eyes widened slightly, and Maya was delighted to see a faint blush rise in his cheeks. She tilted her head up to be kissed. Tanner pressed his lips to hers, and then strode out of the shop.

It was extremely convenient that their new house was just a block west of her new business. Granted, everything in West Tindale was within a few blocks of everything else, but it had made working on the space in the winter much easier. For a few months of every year, it wasn't possible to get anywhere in town without a snowmobile, but the shop was so close that they could walk. From the time they got the keys to their new home in the fall until now, Tanner had poured so much energy into finishing not only the old schoolhouse, but also Maya's soap business, *and* their house.

Anne and Roberto stepped up to the register. Tommy was crying and doing that thing that toddlers do when they arch their backs out of their parents' arms during a tantrum. "It's nap time!" Anne said, speaking over Tommy's cries.

"Also, he's mad because I stopped him from eating a candle," Roberto added.

Maya laughed. "Take that little monster home," she said. "Thank you for coming."

"Always," Anne replied. "And we'll be at Poetry Night at Sullivan's tomorrow. Thanks for hosting there, by the way. Debbie was getting so sick of rearranging the shelves in the bookstore every Tuesday."

"Of course," Maya replied. Tommy let out another wail, this one louder than the ones before. "Go!" Maya said, waving at her friends as they made their way back through the crowd to the door. The next few hours were a blur of ringing up customers, chatting with friends, telling them about the soaps and candles and lip balms and lotions she'd been making all winter.

As the afternoon wore on into evening, and the shop emptied out, Harriet and Bruce came up to Maya. She felt a small twinge of anxiety at their approach—things still weren't perfectly smooth between them, but they were all on speaking terms at this point, which Maya was grateful for.

Harriet reached out a hand and Maya took it. "We're so proud of you, honey," she said.

Tears suddenly stung Maya's eyes. She squeezed her mother's hand. "That means so much to me," she said, her voice tight with emotion.

Bruce stepped in to hug his daughter, and Maya held him extra tightly before pulling away to brush at the tears on her cheeks.

"When is your flight out of Silver Falls tomorrow?" Maya asked.

"We fly out at ten am," Harriet replied. "Then change planes in Salt Lake City, and we don't get to Florida until some ungodly hour at night, but then we'll get right on the cruise ship the next morning."

Maya grinned. "You're taking well to retirement," she said.

Bruce put his arm around his wife. "That was always the plan."

None of them talked about how the other details of their plan had fallen through—their children inheriting and running the hotel, but it felt like all of the Clarks had landed where they were supposed to. Devan was working at a game store in Silver Falls, and after much debate,

Harriet and Bruce had sold their hotel to a chain and were using the money they made from the sale to travel the world. Maya was sure that her parents' decision was a tough one. Everything about it still felt a little tender to her. But there was a peace, there, too.

After Tanner had brought her phone cord, he had stuck around and chatted with everyone until the last customer had filed out the door. Maya closed the curtains, locked the door, and collapsed onto the soft new carpet. She stared at the ceiling. Tanner lowered himself down to lay beside her.

"How do you feel?" he asked.

"Exhausted," Maya replied.

"But happy?"

Maya turned her face toward Tanner. "So happy," she said. "I have a super-hot boyfriend and the best friends a girl could ask for and my own little shop in West Tindale. It's everything I ever wanted."

Tanner got up onto one elbow so that he could look down at her. Then he leaned over and pressed his lips to her jaw. He rose up and ran a finger down the side of her face. "You're everything I ever wanted," he whispered.

Maya looked into his hazel eyes and reached up to brush one of his curls out of his face. Then she pulled on his collar, bringing his face to hers so that she could kiss him. Tanner deepened their kiss, rolling his body over hers. It wasn't the first time they made out in the soap shop, and it definitely wouldn't be the last.

Tanner brushed his lips against Maya's. "What do you want, Maya Clark?" he whispered.

She reached up and put her hands around his neck. When she answered, it was through a grin she could barely contain. "You," she said.

Acknowledgments

Special thanks to Mikah Whittaker, Sam Baird, Amber Taylor, and Andy Hansen for being incredible beta readers. Your insights helped shape this book into a deeper and truer story.

Thank you to Ellie Otis for making sure all my words were in the right places, and for your friendship in general.

Thank you to the cast of *Pride and Prejudice* at The Grand Theater 2024, for problem-solving discussions on how to conceal erections.

Thanks to IHOP, always, for being one of my favorite writing places.

Thank you to Sean Sweeney, whose idea of a "want list" drove so much of this story.

Shout out to the incredible writing communities on social media, who continue to inspire and guide me.

Thank you to the romance writers who keep teaching me to be a better writer and storyteller myself.

My deepest gratitude to those who read the first book in this series and gave it so much love, especially Lily Wariner, Chase McKnight, Brittany Sherwood, and Amy Whitcomb (my love for you is deep); Dava Tuttle, Michelle Blum, Amanda Kerth Roselip, and my family. Your praise gave me the encouragement I needed to keep writing.

And finally, thanks to all the readers, everywhere. I'm convinced that every person who reads is magic.

Also by Elle Whittaker

WEST TINDALE

Halfway to You (August 2025)

Halfway Through the Holidays

ROCK ROMANCES

Rules Worth Breaking (July 2025)

Kisses Worth Waiting For (October 2025)

ENCOUNTERS

Under His Hands

At Your Service

OTHER THINGS

Jane Eyre and Zombies

About the Author

Elle Whittaker is the pen name for Liz Whittaker, who is the daughter of a poem and an ancient Egyptian hieroglyph. She spent most of her time on the shores of Neverland before moving to Salt Lake City, where she currently lives in a library until she can afford an RV. Her heart alternates between pumping lemonade and ink. Her favorite foods are music and knowledge, which she eats as often as possible from atop her mountain of crippling student debt. Her other job is theatre. In her free time, she enjoys hugging trees, doing jigsaw puzzles, going on walks, and thinking about outer space. She is happily a victim of the kind of moonstruck madness that drives her to not only write romance novels, but poetry, scripts, essays, and theatre reviews under various names.

instagram.com/ellewhittakerromance

tiktok.com/@elle.whittaker.romance

www.ingramcontent.com/pod-product-compliance
Lightning Source LLC
Chambersburg PA
CBHW061525310726
48972CB00008B/2324